DEAD KIDS TELL NO TALES

DEAD KIDS TELL NO TALES

STEVE BROWN

Chick Springs Publishing
Taylors, SC

First published in the USA in 2000 by
Chick Springs Publishing
PO Box 1130, Taylors, SC 29687
e-mail: ChickSprgs@aol.com
website: www.chicksprings.com

Library of Congress Control Number:
00-133402
Library of Congress Data Available

ISBN: 0-9670273-4-9

10   9   8   7   6   5   4   3   2

For John D. MacDonald

ACKNOWLEDGMENTS

I would like to thank the usual reading group for their help:
Missy Johnson, Mark Brown, Chris Roerden, Ellen Smith,
and Cathy Wiggins and Lesta Sue Hardee of the
Chapin Memorial Library.
Also, Private Detective Timothy R. Simmons,
and my favorite Generation Xer, Stacey, for
making me sound slightly hip, and, of course, Mary Ella.

"Me wrong?…I don't think so."
—Susan Chase

AUTHOR'S NOTE

Although the cities, locations, and organizations mentioned in this book are real, any references to them, characters, and events are for the purpose of entertainment only and are part of a fictional account.

1

It was January and cold as a bitch along the Grand Strand when my boyfriend dropped a bomb on me. Chad and I were lying in front of a fire at the time, watching the flickers of a gas fireplace. I was baby-sitting my godchild, a child who was soon to go missing and cause me to lose my religion. I lay in Chad's arms—skin on skin—and felt cozy, not just from the fire, but because of Chad.

I think I've been in love with Chad Rivers ever since the day he stopped by my lifeguard stand. Myrtle Beach is the town Hurricane Hugo missed, leveling Charleston instead. That sucker tried to blow some of those snobs out to sea. Too bad it wasn't more successful.

Anyway, back to Chad. I always come back to Chad, even when I'm kidnapped and sold into white slavery. I'll always come back because the guy is absolutely dreamy. And if the dreamy part appears a bit much, remember I'm in my twenties and still allowed a few illusions, especially about the man I love.

We were baby-sitting for Donna Destefani. Donna and I went to school together, what little school I attended. I first mentioned my godchild to Chad a few weeks after we'd met.

In front of another fire. We were roasting oysters and Chad hadn't believed a word I'd said.

"The tough-as-nails Susan Chase has a godchild? How is that possible?"

"Donna asked and I qualified."

"Qualified?"

"As a Catholic. Donna and I go way back. We went to Socastee High together."

"I didn't think you went to high school."

"I did." I sat up and found one of his knees to lean against. "I was a freshman for a while."

Chad's easy to lean into. He's a tall fellow, and you have to be tall to tower over my five-feet-ten. Chad has broad shoulders, narrow hips, and a tight little butt. Narrow face with a mop of brown hair always in a mess: ragged cut, ends over the ears, and down his neck. "For a while, you were?"

"Until my father fell overboard and drowned and they sent me off to that damn foster home."

"Susan, you said you'd work on your swearing." With a smile, he added, "You know how much my mother hates foul language."

"Your mother grew up on Easy Street, not on the mean streets."

"She only wants the best for her baby."

"And you've got it," I said, turning myself into him.

As Chad reached for my breasts and my nipples reached for him, I heard the baby stir. I leaped to my feet and bolted from the room. Running down the hall, I grabbed the door molding and swung myself into the room, then tiptoed over to her crib.

Megan was asleep. My godchild was dark-complected and had black hair. She reminded me of her dead father, a man who also had very dark eyes and who had come to a rather violent end.

When I returned, Chad asked, "What's the problem? You were out of here like a shot."

"She's okay. She's sleeping."

"Susan, you're hyper about this kid."

I rejoined him on the floor. "I'm her godmother."

"And you always imagine the worst."

Swinging my leg around to straddle him, I said, "Believe me, buddy boy, it doesn't take much imagination where I come from."

Chad leaned back, hands behind his back, his, er, manhood staring me right in the eye. "I don't stand a chance, do I? Any little criticism is laughed off, then it's on to the next subject."

"No sense in dwelling on the past."

"I must admit you certainly have a strong self-image for a girl who raised herself."

"Girl?" I said, throwing out my chest.

"Okay. Woman. Full-grown woman, in this case."

"And just as tasty," I said with a wicked smile.

"You were how old when your father died—sixteen?"

"Fifteen." I gazed into the fire and wrapped my arms around my knees.

My father had been a drunk, and on occasion had hit my mother, until she finally walked out on us. Maybe dear ol' Mom thought she'd give me a taste of being the target of such abuse. I never understood what I did to set Daddy off. I shivered and it wasn't from the weather outside the apartment complex where Donna Destefani and her daughter lived.

Chad pulled me into him. "Bad vibes?" he asked.

"Daddy. Visiting again."

"I shouldn't have mentioned it. You know, Suze, you're not as tough as you think you are."

"You know," I said, slipping into his arms, "I sure as hell don't want to be."

"Susan, please."

"What I meant to say was: 'I sure don't want to be.' Or 'I sure as heck don't want to be' or 'I shore don't wanna be.'" I turned my cheek up for a kiss.

3

After giving me my reward, he said, "I'd say you're making progress. Slowly but surely."

We sat in silence, staring into the flames and listening for the baby. I was trying to listen. Chad was nibbling on my ear and I was ready to surrender.

"What's this business about checking on Megan all the time—trying to show me your feminine side?"

"No. I save that just for you."

"Still, it's hard to get your mind around something like Susan Chase's feminine side. Last I heard she broke up a white slavery ring. Before that she drowned the leading suspect in a murder case."

I blinked away the drowsiness my boyfriend had induced in me. "You have me confused with someone else, sir. I only look for runaways."

I'm a lifeguard at Myrtle Beach. My side business began when a father approached me about finding his son. I'd been recommended by the local gendarmes. And the father had pictures and money. Five hundred dollars. He wanted me to go searching places where a parent couldn't get in, or at best, would be blown off.

People would pay for this? And I could look after pulling my shift at the beach? Nice work if you can find it. So, the next day I laid out of my regular job and worked the police stations, telling cops to send me all those worried parents. I reached the point where if a parent wouldn't pay in advance, I wouldn't go looking. Still, even when I took their money, many jobs didn't pan out. Some kids didn't deserve to be found, and many times I'd had to return the money and find a shelter or contact a grandparent. I'd done less and less searching for runaways when Chad Rivers walked into my life.

Chad's father builds boats in Conway, where the land's cheaper and Mr. Rivers can keep more of the profit for his family. Indirectly for me, if I married the boy. But there was a distance between Chad and me, one that Chad thought he understood.

4

"So how'd you become a godparent?" asked that boyfriend, drawing me back to the here and now.

I sat up. "You don't know how it's done?"

"Humor me. I'm a Baptist."

"Well, most denominations don't have godparents. The Episcopal Church treats the ceremony as a social function but not Catholics. You practically have to be born into the church to be a godparent, and I had to go through a ton of stuff to qualify. When the priest learned my grandparents, on my mother's side, had been Catholic, I was in. Except I had to go to confirmation classes to renew my faith. That was a real trip, for the priest, myself, and the other members of the class." I grinned. "Lucky for Megan she wasn't born a boy and Jewish. Ten people have to watch the baby's circumcision."

"Ouch," complained Chad, losing some of his strength. He returned my smile. "I'm not sure my mother would allow me to marry a Catholic."

That was Chad's problem. Mrs. Rivers was from Charleston and thought she was better than most. Yes, yes, I know. A lot of folks in Charleston need to get a life. Chad's mother married down, meaning she married a guy who had ideas and could make money. Money doesn't count for anything in Charleston unless it's old money, so Mrs. Rivers has been working her butt off to elevate the family's position. And her precious baby had gone and fallen for a lifeguard. It wasn't something you could brag about at the Junior League.

I'd visited their awesome house but had little interest in the place—after we'd done the dirty deed in his parents' bed. After that, I only cared to drop by and smirk. And I halfway figured Chad's mom knew what the smirk was all about. Who knows? The security's fairly tight around that place. They have cameras.

"Are you legally bound—as a godparent?"

"Chad, you've been spending too much time around your father's attorneys."

"A boat builder can't have too many lawyers."

"Now you sound like your father."

"I thought you liked him."

"I do, but he wants me to go back to school."

"You can understand—my father received his degree before he started building boats. I did, too."

"Another test I have to pass."

"Suze, you don't have to pass any tests for me. You don't have to do anything." He wrapped his arms around me. "I like you just the way you are."

"It would sound so much better if you had said 'I love you just the way you are.'"

"You know I do."

"Yes, but it would be nice to hear from time to time that you love me."

"Susan, I do love you."

"No, no," I said, disengaging myself from him. "You have to say it without prompting."

"I don't have to be prompted to tell you I love you."

"Jeez, I liked this conversation better when I was explaining godparenting."

"I've never heard about it, unless it was in fairy tales."

"It's much more high church."

"High church?"

"Yeah—incense, ceremony, and lots of robes that could pull double duty as church drapery."

"There's more to it than you've told me?"

"Stand up in a ceremony and tell them I'd be a good girl." He laughed. "Susan, don't tell me you lied in church."

"No, dummy," I said, slapping his arm. "About taking my responsibilities seriously about being a godparent."

He rubbed his arm. "You hit pretty good."

"For a girl, you mean."

"I didn't mean—"

"I swim in the Waterway every day."

"This time of year?"

"Start the first of April."

"Then," he said, tightening his grip on me, "since it's not even February and you're still in a weakened state, I can take advantage of you."

With a sigh, I said, "I was wondering when we'd get around to that."

We were in the middle of something really nice when I heard the baby again. I rolled from under Chad, leaped to my feet, and ran naked down the hallway. Grabbing the molding, I swung myself into the room again. Tiptoeing over to the crib, I saw my sweet baby sleeping peacefully.

Chad stood at the door—naked. "What is it this time?"

I pulled the blanket up to her cute little chin. Didn't want my little precious to catch a cold. Megan gurgled, smiled, and continued to sleep away.

"You know, Susan, I don't think I'll try making love to you while you're baby-sitting."

We left the room, both buck naked and arm in arm. "It's probably for the best."

"For the worst from my point of view," he said, glancing down.

I gripped him lower than his waist. "Give me another chance, pretty please. I'll concentrate this time."

He gasped. "But don't you think we should do it outside Megan's door so you can hear her cry—if she actually does?"

I squeezed again and he yelped. It was a moment before he could fully concentrate on me again.

Later, when we were lying in each other's arms, Chad dropped his bombshell. Usually all this screwing around happens at my place, which happens to be an old shrimp boat.

Daddy's Girl is moored along the Intracoastal Waterway, a series of canals, sheltered bays, and channels extending three thousand miles up and down the Atlantic coast. The Intracoastal was built to protect small craft from the perils of the ocean, and living there is a damn sight cheaper than any place on the beach.

Chad said, "I guess I'd best be getting along."

"Oh, yes, now that you've finished with me, sir, you toss me aside like some used doll."

Chad pulled on his underwear. "You know, I think there's something to all those challenges you throw at me."

"I didn't know I was that much of a challenge." I stood, naked as a jaybird, and looked for my underwear.

"It's in just about everything you say. A guy can only take so much." He pulled on his pants.

I reached for my panties. "What are you trying to tell me? Something you feel more comfortable saying with pants on?"

"I think we should go for counseling."

"Counseling?" I'd been hopping around, trying to put a leg down my jeans. I stopped, one leg in, one leg out. "Counseling's for married couples."

"Sometimes people who're considering the next step . . . ."

"I didn't know we were considering the next step. Why, you don't even know my favorite color."

"Because you joke about everything, like you're doing now."

"Where did you get the idea we needed counseling?"

He found his shirt. "Mother said if you and I are serious we should enter counseling to see if there's anything to be serious about."

"I'm uncomfortable about this coming from your mom."

"It didn't come from my mother—"

"But you said—"

"Susan, if you'll give me a chance to explain."

I snatched up my bra and turned my back on him, pulling the garment around me and hooking it on. My blouse was around here somewhere.

"We've only known each other six months and already we're having these problems."

"I don't have any problem—"

"Susan, are you going to let me finish?"

"Yes," I said through clenched teeth, my back still to him, making it impossible to locate my blouse. My eyes ached. At any minute I might burst into tears. What was up with that?

"I'm not sure how it's been for other guys—"

"Pretty fucking good. From what they've said."

Chad sighed. "There you go again."

"What?" I asked, facing him, "interrupting or cursing?"

"You know, if you didn't have a sense of humor, I don't see how anyone could stand you."

"Maybe you're not tough enough—"

Chad's hand came up. "Don't go there. I may be tougher than you think."

I watched that hand. "You wouldn't—"

"Don't be silly, Suze." He lowered his hand. "I'd never hit you."

"I would hope not."

"Susan!"

I shut up.

"I'm tough enough to walk away and never see you again—is that tough enough?"

"You'd do that?"

"I just want a chance"—he smiled—"to finish a sentence."

"So what are you trying to tell me?"

"I don't want to lose you, Suze, but all this pent-up hostility . . . ." He put a finger on my lips so I would remember to keep my frigging mouth shut. "Toward people, toward the whole world. It's a major jones for you."

When he took his finger away, I said, "I had a rough childhood and grew up not trusting anyone."

"You don't trust me?"

I looked around for my blouse. "I'm learning to trust you." There I was again, being so blunt nobody could stand me but my closest friends, and it goes without saying that I don't have many close friends. "I don't need to see a shrink.

I already have one: Dads."

Dads is what I call my sixty-some-odd-year-old neighbor whose schooner is moored beside *Daddy's Girl*. "Dads" isn't his real name. It's Harry Poinsett. Harry's a descendant of the fellow who christened the scarlet-leafed plant you decorate your house with at Christmas, but I prefer "Dads." Dads says it implies intimacy without being close. Harry says stuff like that. He's a retired diplomat who took early retirement to sail up and down the Waterway, rarely venturing out to sea. Like Dads says, when you've seen it all, seeing it twice just wouldn't be the same. Dads knows the school system gave short shrift to my generation, so he's tried to educate me. Generation X was expected to learn the new math in open classrooms, fill in the blanks when it came to sex and drugs, and never think how lucky we'd been to have survived the Pill.

"Susan, you really don't trust me?"

"We're supposed to tell each other the truth. We agreed— remember?"

"You're so straight about everything . . . ."

"I'm not going to see a shrink. Take me as I am."

"I have." He sat down and slipped on a sock, then reached for a shoe. "I just wish there was a third party involved, someone neutral."

"There's Dads."

Chad pulled on a shoe, one of those half boots that looks like a climbing shoe but would break your ankle if you tried to climb in it. "Talking to Harry would be like our talking to my mother."

"Dads has had plenty of experience negotiating with hostile parties. He's a former diplomat."

"But we're not hostile, and I really wouldn't want Harry to think you and I were having problems. You wouldn't want to give my mother any leverage, would you?"

"Dads would never do that."

"I don't know him like you do." After lacing up the boot,

he said, "Susan, it bothers me that you don't trust me."

"You want me to lie?"

He picked up another sock. "Of course not."

"I think you're worried about nothing. We've gotten the sex out of the way and found there's no problem there. I'd say we're right where we should be: talking about the in-laws and whether I'll ever get a regular job and be able to handle my end of the bargain." Looking at him from under my eyebrows, I asked, "Would there be something else?"

He pulled on his second boot and laced it. "Everything pales next to your hostility."

"I'm not sure I can live with your mom's hostility—toward me."

"I don't think that's fair."

"Most girls would make you choose between your mother and your girlfriend. I haven't done that. You want to do stuff with your family. I go along. I don't make waves."

"At least you could look like you were enjoying yourself."

"I don't fit in. Your mother knows it, and I hope to God you never figure it out."

Chad smiled that little boy smile of his that turns my legs to jelly. I really cared for this guy and I didn't want to lose him. I'd never met a guy like Chad Rivers.

He stood, taking me into his arms. "God, but you are some piece of work."

"God should know. He allowed me to become Megan's godmother."

Chad laughed and said to give counseling some thought. At the door he kissed me, and thinking I heard Megan again, I left him there. When I returned, the door was closed and my boyfriend was gone.

2

A week later I returned to Donna's for my Saturday babysitting gig. Driving over, I wondered why I hadn't been able to put Chad's suggestion of counseling out of my mind. I'd grown up in one coastal town after another, and most of my friends had been adults. All of them, to a man—another of my problems—wanted me to go back to school, get a job, and meet the right guy. Then I could have the marriage, the children, the mortgage, and the dental plan. Marriage to Chad Rivers would change all that. I wouldn't have to scuffle for a living, our children would attend the best schools, and the mortgage on our home would be on a house I never would've dreamed of owning. And the dental plan—oh, who the hell worries about the damn dental plan when you have money like the Rivers family.

Anyway, Lois Rivers had grown up with money. Rather, her father inherited a bunch of land, and instead of being a good little rich boy and spending his days drinking and his nights trying to seduce his neighbors' wives, he became aware of the residential building boom around Charleston. Lois' father developed the family holdings into a series of middle-class subdivisions and had more than one deal in the air when the real estate market came to a standstill. You can pinpoint that moment in time. It was when the Baby Boomers realized they couldn't upgrade to the next larger house size and began to watch *This Old House* to learn how to be satisfied with their lot in life. A satisfied Boomer. What an oxymoron.

Lois' father used something else handed down from generation to generation: a dueling pistol, with which he blew out his brains. Creditors descended on the operation, and when they'd finished picking it clean—Lois' father had had a heart condition and been a poor insurance risk—her family was left with only their house. The home was saved because Lois' mother had refused to allow it to be mortgaged. So when Chad's father proposed marriage, Lois quickly agreed, preferring to live with her husband's dreams than in nouveau poverty in Charleston. As far as I knew, Lois had little contact with her family.

I learned about Lois' family when I had some free time after locating a runaway in Charleston. Not that I was ticked at Lois. Not at all. What sent me on this line of investigation was becoming a godparent. It changes your frigging life.

Megan's mom and I were competitors at two-man volleyball before Donna went off to pharmacy school. There she fell for an engineer—because he reprimanded his workmen for catcalling the passing females on their way to class. It was love at first sight, not to mention the bod on Robert Destefani could make a girl weak in the knees. Robert threatened to use those muscles on his construction crew if they weren't more respectful to the women passing the job site. Come to think of it, I could've gone for a guy like that.

A year after Megan was born, one of Robert's men backed a cherry picker—one of those machines with a boom topped off by a bucket—into a high tension wire. Very quickly several zillion volts were running through the poor guy. Throwing himself through the cab, Robert was able to knock the guy out of the chair, but he was electrocuted when his foot caught on the gear shift and he was pulled to the floor. Suddenly Donna was a widow with a degree in pharmacy and a small child to raise. There were no grandparents on her side, no brothers or sisters, so I whipped down with a U-Haul, and before the weekend was over, had Donna and Megan housed in the Pirate's Cove, a two-story apartment complex just off the beach. At the time I thought it a safe enough place to raise any kid.

Her father-in-law was actually relieved at not being responsible for another child. Mrs. Destefani had third-stage Alzheimer's and didn't remember her husband or her son. The poor woman was spared the misery of his death, but her husband's life became a living hell. Mr. Destefani could remember everything, even their hopes and dreams for their son. And me? I'd pitched in and helped because I'd been blown away when Donna had asked me to be her child's godmother.

I stepped down from my jeep at the Pirate's Cove and didn't lock up. All that's inside is a footlocker where a back seat should be. I have everything in that footlocker, including supplies for several days of being away from home looking for runaways. From the footlocker I took a box wrapped in white paper and decorated with a pink ribbon. Inside was a new jumper I proudly carried upstairs.

Opening the door with my own key, I called, "It's Susan." Megan was going to look way neat in . . . .

Donna rushed into the living room with Megan under one arm, her purse and her cold weather coat in the other. The sight of Megan being carried like a sack of potatoes always startles me. Donna has a wiry frame and lots of energy. She can flat-out fill prescriptions.

Her blue eyes flashed. "You forgot, didn't you?"

"I thought I was early." I held out the gift. "I've got something for the baby."

"Put it on her yourself. I've got to run."

"You don't want to open it?"

"I'm late. I've got to go."

"Late?"

"I was transferred to Garden City. Remember?" Garden City was half an hour down the coast from where Donna lived. "I don't mean to be harsh, Susan, but when you have children you'll understand. My job has to come first—to take care of Megan."

"It won't happen again," I said rather lamely.

"Yes, yes," she replied, looking around and not listening to me.

Flashing a big smile, I said, "But you have to admit I've never missed a chance to be with my godchild."

Donna saw her keys on the window between the living room and the kitchen. "No, but you have been late before." She handed me the baby. Megan didn't like that and let out a yowl.

After snatching up her keys, Donna slid into her coat. "Think you should sit today? I can call someone else."

I clutched the whimpering child to my chest. "I don't know why you should."

"You don't look too happy about it."

"I'm just embarrassed."

She patted my arm as she headed for the door. "Then I'm sure everything will be just fine. The number's on the refrigerator."

"I know the number, Donna."

"I mean the new one."

Before she could grasp the knob, the door opened and another woman stepped into the apartment. The young woman appeared to be a little older than me, with short brown hair, so short you could see a sharp pair of ears laid back against her head.

"Oh," she said, pocketing her keys. "Your friend arrived." Her face was round, her eyes brown, and her lips very narrow.

She wore jeans, running shoes, and a sweatshirt with Rutledge College emblazoned across the front. The sweatshirt covered a stocky frame.

"Yes, yes." Donna glanced at her hands as if reminding herself she had her keys and handbag. "She finally got here."

I gritted my teeth but said nothing, just held the baby tighter. Thankfully, Megan had stopped crying.

"Susan, why don't you two get acquainted. Babe's had tons of experience baby-sitting, even in college."

So, after putting me in my place about not only baby-sitting skills, but also my lack of education, my friend was out the door, closing it behind her.

"Babe?"

"It's a nickname. Daddy gave it to me. He never did like 'Constance' or 'Delphine.'"

"Your parents named you that?"

"My mother. It's awful, isn't it?"

"No, but pretty close."

"I don't know what she had in mind. I mean 'Constance' means constant and 'Delphine' means calmness. I certainly don't fit that description. I tend to be more excitable. Maybe Daddy knew something, calling me 'Babe,' but my mother always called me 'Constance.' It was her mother's name."

So I was left with Constance Delphine Parnell, or "Babe," who I quickly learned was not only friendly but talkative. That was cool with me. I wanted to know who this woman was and why Donna had given her a key to the apartment. She might not even be Catholic.

Babe told me everything as she warmed a bottle for Megan. Sandwiches and iced tea followed. No wonder she'd usurped my position. I could use someone like her around my boat.

"Are you a local?" she asked.

I nodded and clutched the baby. Parnell wasn't getting that job. I loved feeding Megan.

Babe handed me the bottle, then glanced out the window. "I never knew it could be so dismal at the beach."

That wasn't so unusual. Many people think if they move to the Grand Strand, a year-round job will follow, along with plenty of South Florida weather.

Parnell sliced the crust off four slices of rye bread, then placed our lunch on plates from Donna's wedding collection. "But I'm determined to make the best of it."

"Your parents didn't approve of the move?"

"My parents?" The woman stopped pouring the tea. "My parents are old fogies. Don't you find that to be true of your parents?"

"My parents are deceased, I think."

"You think?"

"Well, both disappeared."

Parnell ignored her food. She'd made two ham on ryes, and I don't remember her asking me what I wanted. She sat down. "Tell me all about it, Susan."

"Nothing to tell," I said, rocking the baby and feeding her the bottle at the same time. "My father drowned at sea. A few years earlier my mother walked out on us."

"You were there when your father drowned?"

"Yes."

"And you couldn't save him?"

"It happened while I was below. Asleep."

She nodded as if understanding, but what could anyone understand about the night I lost my father. It was the same night I'd killed someone. You never forget the first—or the second, or the third, for that matter.

"It must be sad, carrying all that guilt."

"What guilt?"

"About not being able to save your father. What do you do for family?"

"I have a friend who thinks he's my grandfather. And I baby-sit for Donna. I haven't seen you before. Where'd you say you were from?"

Babe smiled across the plate where her untouched sandwich lay. "Don't mind me, Susan. I just wanted to meet people and Donna was my bridge."

"Don't you miss home?" It was what all the kids talked about when living at the beach: home. Go figure.

"Home is . . . ." Babe paused, as if considering what to say. "Home is Waxhaw, North Carolina, a town on the North Carolina/South Carolina border. It's Andrew Jackson's birthplace. But nobody's interested in history these days. Don't you find that to be true, that no one's much interested in the past? I spend a lot of time in graveyards, but people don't want to hear about that."

"Graveyards?" I glanced at Megan, wondering if this was something the baby should hear.

Parnell nodded. "I make tombstone rubbings with graphite until the image on the stone appears. It's a hobby."

"Oh."

"Both North and South Carolina claim Andrew Jackson, but the fact is he was born in his uncle's house, not his own home, and that house was on the west side of the road so he couldn't've been born in North Carolina."

"He couldn't?" was all I could say, sucked into a conversation I couldn't follow.

"The road between Jackson's home and his uncle's was the border between North and South Carolina, so you see," she said with a broad smile, "Jackson couldn't have been born in North Carolina."

"If he was born in his uncle's house, you mean." History never was my strong suit, or any other subject.

"Well, he was."

"How do you know?" I really wanted to know. What people run off at the mouth about is usually the key to understanding them. Babe Parnell appeared a little wacky and she had access to my godchild.

"Jackson said so in his papers."

"You've read them?"

"Oh, no," she said with a laugh. "I only know a fact here and there. Just enough to toss out at cocktail parties."

"You go to a good number of those?"

The woman noticed the plate in front of her. She picked up her sandwich, took a bite, and chewed it thoroughly. "It's just a phrase. People aren't interested in history. It's a way to blow them off—in the nicest way."

"Can you blame them? It's really dull."

Babe put down her sandwich. "That's where you're wrong. What you learned in school was a sanitized version used to sell textbooks. No one cares for controversy and that's why history's such a bore."

"But all history is conflict—the Civil War, the Revolutionary War? It was all about conflict."

"Gosh, Susan, it's really nice to meet someone who actually reads."

Oh, shit! What had I gotten myself into?

"What'd you hate about history when you were in school?"

"It's all dates and places. You memorize a bunch of boring stuff."

"Then you get out of school and learn there's more, like when you read those history books you mentioned."

There hadn't been many of those. Most of them Dads forced on me. The latest was *Robert the Bruce: King of Scots*. Harry said I should know something about my ancestors. I was halfway through the book before I realized the Scots didn't have godchildren. They were all Protestants.

"Do you remember the Alamo?" asked Parnell.

Of course. John Wayne was in the movie. And Wyatt Earp. There were plenty of movies about him.

The woman was a mind reader. "Wyatt Earp. Know who he was?"

"Yes."

"And the Lost Colony?"

"*The Lost Colony* is a tourist trap in North Carolina." Taking the bottle from the baby's mouth, I laid Megan on my shoulder and burped her. "What's this? A pop quiz?"

"Bear with me, Susan. Do you know why the colony was

lost in the first place?"

"Er—Indians massacred everyone?"

"Not really. When the ships from England failed to return, the colonists joined the Indians and turned their backs on England. That's not something you'll read in a textbook." Parnell leaned forward. "Do you remember what they fought for at the Alamo?"

"Er—freedom. From Mexico."

"I'm not trying to embarrass you, but do you remember who Wyatt Earp really was?"

Was this a trick question?

"Don't make it so hard on yourself. Just say the first thing that comes to mind."

"He was a lawman. Some kind of sheriff."

"Actually Earp wasn't a sheriff, but that's not the point. At the Alamo the men who fought there—"

"Davy Crockett and Jim Bowie," I said proudly.

"Yes." Babe smiled indulgently, and her smile stretched all the way to the corners of her mouth, accentuating the pointiness of her ears. "Travis, Bowie, and Crockett—all were fighting for slavery."

"Slavery?"

"To make Texas into a slave state."

"Are you sure about that?" I didn't remember that from the movies.

"If you wanted to become a citizen of the Mexican Republic, which Texas was at the time, you had to become a member of the Catholic Church, swear allegiance to the Mexican government, and give up slavery."

I glanced at the baby. All this history talk had put Megan to sleep. "Excuse me."

I took the baby down the hall and laid her in her crib. I pulled a coverlet over her chest, just below her chin. She looked so sweet sleeping there.

Parnell was washing up when I returned, arms of the Rutledge College sweatshirt shoved up above her elbows.

"Did she wake up?" she asked from the sink.

"No problem."

"I wasn't sure. You were gone so long."

"She's okay. I know how to take care of her."

I went into the living room, picked up the gift, and took it down the hall. I wasn't about to unwrap it. I'd leave that to Donna. Returning to the table, I ate my ham on rye with little conversation. I had to find a way to get rid of this woman or it was going to be a very long afternoon.

Parnell returned the wedding plate she had used to the cupboard, sat down, and sipped her iced tea. "So, when the Americans extended slavery into Mexico, it caused the fight at the Alamo."

"Maybe they didn't want to become Catholics."

Parnell giggled. "That's funny, that Texas fought for its independence because they didn't want to become Catholics. But it's not true. Just like Wyatt Earp was on both sides of the law when it suited him. Hollywood made Earp into a hero and Hollywood doesn't mention slavery at the Alamo. You wouldn't sell many textbooks in Texas."

"Selling textbooks in Texas is that important?"

"Susan, the Texas Board of Education practically controls what's in American textbooks. But people aren't interested in knowing such things, like South Carolina was first settled by black people. That wouldn't go over very well in Charleston, would it?"

She had that right.

"If it's mentioned at all, it's passed over quickly, moving on to the accomplishments of white people." Babe took a sip of tea. "I've been thinking of writing a paper on it, but why? It wouldn't sell."

"Sell?"

"That's what I do for a living. Sell fillers and articles about the South to national and regional magazines. It doesn't pay all that well, but it makes it possible to see the country."

"You like moving from place to place?" My family had done

that and I wouldn't wish it on anyone.

"Let's just say things haven't always worked out." Finished with her tea, Babe went to the sink where she washed out her glass and put it in the drainer. "So what do you and Megan have planned this afternoon?"

"Thought we'd just hang. Maybe go outside. Before it gets dark."

Babe glanced through the window over the sink. "In this weather?"

"Babies can go out in any weather if you dress them properly." I didn't explain this was something Donna had taught me. I'd been scared to take Megan outside. Of course, rainy days were strictly taboo.

"I wouldn't know. I've never had a baby. I came close, but I never met the right guy."

More to myself than Parnell, I said, "I wonder if I have."

"Now don't tell me a cute girl like yourself hasn't got a boyfriend. You may be big, but you do have a good figure, and you're blond."

"I guess I do, the boyfriend, I mean."

"What's he like?"

I told her about Chad, more than I should've. Probably out of frustration.

"Counseling? He must be really serious."

"I think he's serious about making me normal."

"Normal?" Babe glanced in the direction of the baby's room. "What's abnormal about you? You look okay to me." She laughed a little too quickly.

"I don't aspire to the suburban life: PTA, carpooling, and soccer matches."

"That doesn't sound all that bad to me."

"To each his own. I'm more into dancing all night and two-man volleyball."

"You do that, the volleyball part?"

"Most every day." I glanced at the gloomy window. "Come spring, that is."

"Well, if I get a chance at that kind of life, I'm going to take it. I'm closer to thirty than twenty and time's a wasting, as Snuffy Smith says. When I was doing an article on its creator . . . ."

I thought I heard Megan cry. I got up and hurried down the hall. Megan was wide awake. She lay in her crib, smiling, cooing. Babe came in as I picked up the baby. I checked her diaper, and finding it dry, offered the child to her.

"No, no," said Parnell, pulling down the arms of her sweatshirt, "it's your turn to sit."

"I do it all the time. Plenty during the off-season."

"What do you do?" Her question was only a courtesy because her focus was entirely on the baby, as she took Megan into her arms.

Megan smiled, gurgled, and spit up a bubble of milk.

Well, take that, honey.

Parnell wiped the spot away with the sleeve of her sweatshirt. And me? I literally dropped off her scope. A woman, who had been so interested in what I had to say, completely zoned out on me.

How do I know? For openers I told her about being a lifeguard, which generally gets a girl's attention, but her attention was gone. I returned to the table, finished my ham and rye, then washed the plate, dried it, and put it away. As I did I heard the TV come on. Perhaps Parnell was ready to rejoin the land of the living.

Nope. I found her sprawled on the living room floor, head on a couple of cushions and my godchild in the crook of her arm. She was oblivious to everything, and she continued to ignore me as I sat on the sofa and watched, of all things, educational TV.

All in all it was a pretty miserable afternoon, and after a while, I couldn't take it anymore. Women's basketball would be on soon, on ESPN2, so I told Babe I was going out for something to eat. Would she be here to look after the baby?

Rotating her head, her eyes finally focused on me. "Sure.

Take your time. I'll be here."

I picked up my keys and my fanny pack. "Would you like something?"

"Oh, no. I just had lunch."

"Uh—lunch was five hours ago." Glancing out the window, I could see it was growing dark.

"I'm really not at all hungry."

I was at the door, pulling on my jacket. "If you're going to be here, I'll go to a sports bar, maybe catch a few minutes of the game."

"Game?"

"Tennessee and Connecticut. It's on cable."

The stocky woman raised up on her free arm and looked at me. "But they're about to show a special about the Vietnam War."

Vietnam? I couldn't think of anything more lame. "You want anything or not?"

The woman shook her head and went back to watching TV, arm cradling the baby who had not moved since they'd lain down on the floor hours ago. Well, Donna had given her stamp of approval. Hell, maybe some of that education would rub off on Megan.

When I returned from the sports bar, it was dark outside and the apartment was empty. I know that for a fact because I searched under beds and opened closet doors. Megan had been my responsibility and I'd turned her over to some fool! It didn't matter if the damn fool was a friend of the baby's mother, the damage had already been done.

I left the apartment and raced down the steps before realizing I had no idea which apartment belonged to Parnell. I knocked on the door at the ground floor apartment and no one answered. At the second door the couple didn't know who I was talking about but knew where the resident manager lived. Moments later I was hammering on the resident manager's door. She was a fat woman in a tent dress, her hair in rollers. Through the security chain, she asked, "What can I do for you?"

"Babe Parnell. Which one is her apartment?"

"Sorry, Miss, we don't give out that kind of information."

"But I've got to know."

"And who are you?"

"Susan Chase. A friend."

"Sorry, but if you were Miss Parnell's friend, you'd know which apartment was hers."

"And if I forgot?"

"Perhaps you should call her. There's a phone down the street at the Circle K."

"Why not here?" I asked, looking beyond the woman's curlers and into the apartment. A smell of pasta sauce floated through the cracked door.

"I don't think so."

"Listen, lady, I was baby-sitting for Donna Destefani. Parnell came by. We spent the afternoon together. I went out for food and returned to find the baby gone and no note. I can't remember which unit is Parnell's. She told me, but I can't remember. That must be where she and the baby went."

The fat woman glanced at my hands. "Then where's the food?"

"What?"

"The food you went out for. Where is it?"

"Are you asking for my credentials?"

"You could say that."

Pulling Donna's key from my fanny pack, I asked, "Is this one of your keys?"

"Yes," said the woman, glancing at the key, "but you can't tell whose apartment. That's for security purposes, and why I'm asking these questions. We don't give out residents' apartment numbers to just anyone who asks."

"I'm not just anyone. I'm the child's godparent."

The fat woman sighed. "Okay, I'll call Miss Parnell and see if she's in."

When she returned, she spoke through the chain. "No answer."

"No answer?" My shivers came from more than my missing godchild. Standing in the breezeway, I quickly learned why the open hallway had been given its name. "You don't think she fell down and knocked herself out, do you? She has the baby with her."

"I have no idea—"

"Which apartment is it?"

"Like I said, I can't tell you that."

"But this could be an emergency."

"If you think so, why don't you call 911?"

"Why don't you?"

"Miss Chase, I have better things to do than stand at this door and chat. Now if you don't mind . . . ."

"I'll beat on every door in this fucking complex until I find someone who'll tell me where Babe Parnell lives."

"And I'm within my rights to call the police."

"And I'm responsible for my godchild." Ripping down the side of my fanny pack, the Smith & Wesson fell into my hand. The gun has a shroud on the hammer so it doesn't catch on all the stuff we gals tote around.

The woman gaped at the pistol. "That's a gun."

"No shit. How'd you think I was going to get into Parnell's apartment."

"But you can't do that."

"I'm already doing it," I said, stomping away.

"No, no!" hollered the woman through the crack in the door. "I'll come with you. Just let me get my key. We don't need another incident. There was that boy shooting at sea gulls and the residents got really angry."

No kidding. The kid was probably enticing the birds to come closer by throwing bread crumbs to them.

Two minutes later the chain slid back and the woman

opened the door. She stepped outside in a heavy coat and pulled the door to. She noticed I no longer had my pistol out.

"Thank you for putting away the gun."

"My pleasure."

I followed her to the building housing Donna's apartment. Parnell's place was on the other side, on the top floor. No one answered the door when I knocked.

"Well," I asked, "aren't you going in?"

"I don't know if I should."

"Then give me the key."

"No, no, I'll do it. You stay here."

The woman unlocked the door and called "Miss Parnell" several times from the open doorway.

While I stood in another breezeway shivering from the wind, the bitch took her time walking through the apartment and calling Parnell's name.

"She's not here," she said upon returning.

Damn. Where was that fool?

I darted off, but racing around the complex, I saw no one. In this weather everyone was buttoned up for the night. Dazed, I pulled myself up the railing to Donna's apartment. At the door I stopped, needing a moment to compose myself. Whenever I was in danger, I could usually sort out things, even on the fly, but with Megan missing, I seemed to have lost the ability to focus.

Why the hell had I gone out at all? There'd been plenty of food in the apartment. And Donna would certainly ask if I'd enjoyed flirting with the guys at the sports bar, when I was supposed to be baby-sitting.

I'd had to get out of the apartment because that damned ED-TV had been driving me nuts, and Parnell wouldn't leave. And the baby was asleep.

Well, Susan, if you were this concerned about Babe, why'd you leave Megan with her at all?

For that I had no answer.

Opening the door to the apartment, I saw Babe Parnell lying in the middle of the living room floor with Megan in the crook of her arm. I almost collapsed in relief. It goes without saying that I wasn't in the best shape to explain my condition to a pair of uniformed patrolmen. The cops were there to question me about running around and threatening people with a handgun.

3

"Where the hell have you been?"

"What?" Parnell's eyes were glazed over. She had to focus on me. Could a person become that engrossed in something on ED-TV?

Towering over her, I gulped some air to keep from falling down. "I've been frantic with worry! I come back and you're not here. Neither is the baby. And you're not at your place." I pointed at the window. "It's dark and cold out there. Megan can't be out in that kind of weather."

Parnell slowly got to her feet, and as she did, brought the child along. "Susan, are you all right?"

"No. I'm pissed. I want to know where you've been."

"We were outside. When you left, I thought about what you'd said about babies being able to go outside. I went into the bedroom and dressed Megan warmly and took her outside. There was nothing wrong with that. You said so yourself."

"Except I couldn't find you! Or Megan. And you didn't leave a note. I didn't see you anywhere and I went all around this damn place."

"Susan, there's no reason for that kind of language. We're

fine. Are you sure you're all right?"

"I'm not worried about me! I was worried about my god-child."

"And I told you. We were outside."

"Where?"

"Susan, really, you need to calm down." Parnell glanced at Megan clutching her chest. "You're upsetting the baby."

"I want to know!"

"Like I tried to tell you—"

There was a knock at the door and the baby uttered a small cry. I stood there for a moment, then shook myself like a dog coming out of water.

It was two cops: a thin black one and a chubby white one, both from the Myrtle Beach Police Department.

"Oh, that's just fucking great. Now that we don't need you. The damn fool's back with the baby. She'd been outside with her."

The black cop asked, "Are you Miss Chase?"

"Yes. I'm the baby-sitter."

"Miss Chase, could you come downtown with us?"

"What the hell for? I don't need to make any report. The baby's back." I gestured over my shoulder. "She's just fine." That was right. I was the one rattled.

"Miss Chase, if you could watch your language—"

"I hear that all the damn time. Could we plow some new ground?"

The white cop hitched up his equipment belt. "Ma'am, is it true you were brandishing a pistol around the apartment complex?"

"Brandishing?" I felt the remainder of my energy drain away.

"Yes, threatening people with a gun."

"Miss Chase," said the black cop, "you'll have to come downtown and answer some questions."

"But—but I'm baby-sitting."

The black man looked beyond me to Parnell. "Miss, are

you willing to care for the baby while we talk with Miss Chase downtown?"

Parnell nodded and clutched the baby to her chest. Megan began to whimper.

"I'm not leaving her with the baby."

"Why not? I baby-sit for Megan all the time. Besides, I'm not all that comfortable with Megan being around someone . . . with a gun."

I took a breath and let it out. "I'll have to call the mother and check with her. I'm the one responsible for the baby, neither of you are, and certainly not this woman."

The black man nodded and stepped into the living room. "But first the pistol."

I untied the fanny pack and handed it to him. It took a moment. My hands shook.

His partner came in and stood beside him, one hand on the butt of his pistol, the other with the thumb inside his belt, feet spread slightly apart. Both men watched me go into the kitchen.

I got Donna on the second ring.

"Donna, this is Susan."

"Yes? Is everything all right?"

"Of course." I cleared my throat. "Why do you ask?"

"You should hear your voice. You sound frantic, and I should know. I get enough calls from mothers about babies. Is Megan okay?"

"Sure." I glanced through the serving window and saw Parnell, jostling and cooing Megan. "Babe is still holding her. She hasn't let go of her since I turned her loose several hours ago."

"Uh-huh. Then what is it?" I could feel Donna drifting back to the world of pills and suppositories.

"I have to go out for a while and I wondered if it would be all right for Babe to sit while I'm gone."

"I don't have any problem with that. Susan, is there a problem with you and Babe?"

"I just wanted to make sure it's okay with you. Babe says she sits for you."

"Yes, yes, she does."

"I just wanted to check."

"Let me speak to Babe."

"She's with the baby."

"Oh, no," said Parnell from the living room. "I can speak to her." She slipped Megan onto her hip and came into the kitchen.

I gave her the phone and got the hell out of there. Before I went out the door, I heard Parnell telling Donna I was being led away by the police.

J.D. Warden was leaving the building as I was led inside the law enforcement center. He saw that my hands were cuffed behind my back.

"What is it this time?" he asked.

And me? Head hunched over, I couldn't speak. All I could think of was that I'd failed Donna and my godchild. I shouldn't've left Megan with that dummy. No wonder Catholics are so picky about godparents.

The black cop told Warden where they'd found me and what I'd been up to. Warden asked if he could speak with me in his office. The two officers looked at each other. The black one nodded, then led me to an office Warden shares with his partner. For some reason Warden thinks he's my Dutch uncle, and maybe this time I needed one.

"Sit." Warden pointed at one of the two metal chairs in front of his desk. Partner DeShields' metal desk faced the wall to my left.

The walls were glass halfway up and on each side were the offices of Myrtle Beach detectives. At the moment these offices were empty. Warden's office had no potted plants or pictures on the wall, but on DeShields' desk sat a few family snaps in shiny, golden frames. Warden's desk was empty but for the "in" and "out" trays. The "out" tray was filled to capacity, the "in" tray empty.

"You know, Chase, I was getting away from this place early for a Saturday."

The cops parked me in a chair, one of them turning over my fanny pack to Warden. When the cuffs came off, my hands flew to my face and I began to sob uncontrollably.

"Chase? Are you all right?"

I wailed and held my face even tighter.

"What happened?" Now he sounded a bit frantic.

"She was in the back of the squad car, sir. We didn't touch her."

"Do you need a matron in here?" asked another nervous voice before the two unforms left.

"No, no. I think she'll be okay. You are going to be all right, aren't you, Chase?"

I nodded. This was not the Susan Chase he was accustomed to—always calm and cool, and with a sharp tongue to keep the cops at bay. I couldn't get it out of my mind that something horrible could've happened to Megan while I'd been gone.

God, this being responsible for another person . . . this sense of helplessness . . . when things spin out of control . . . . It was nothing like I'd ever felt before.

Warden took a seat on the corner of his desk and handed me a Kleenex. A husky man with wide shoulders, dark eyes, and skin that never tans, Warden combs his hair straight back in the style popularized by basketball coach Pat Riley. His shirt is always white on white and the tie maroon; his shoes, wing tips and his socks, dark.

Warden had taken a bullet in the line of duty while working in the Big Apple. Upon learning his daughter's husband would be flying out of Sumter Air Force Base, just down the road from Myrtle Beach, Warden applied for, and received, an appointment to the South Carolina State Law Enforcement Division (SLED: Grand Strand). He and his partner, Mickey DeShields, hold court in the rear of the law enforcement center.

"Chase, what's the problem? I've never seen you like this?"

"I—I almost lost her. She's my godchild and I almost . . . lost her." I needed another Kleenex. This one was damaged beyond repair.

Another came my way. "I thought this was about running around with your Smith & Wesson. I've told you someone would eventually complain. There's a responsibility that goes with carrying any weapon and—"

"I don't give a damn about the pistol!" Tears ran down my face. "I'll get another one! South Carolina is the gun capital of the world."

Warden glanced into the squad room, then left his seat to close the door. "Chase, I want you to calm down. And I want you to think twice before you speak again. Not only do you have charges facing you for pointing and presenting a firearm, but you're threatening to buy an unauthorized firearm."

"But you don't understand. I lost her."

"Plenty of kids disappear and you go looking for them. That's your job. Why is this any different?"

I told him. It took some time, but I finally got it out, with plenty of "the Parnell woman did this" and "the Parnell woman did that." By the time I finished, Warden was sitting beside me and dozens of Kleenex littered the floor. He had a hand on my shoulder and it didn't bother me. Matter of fact, it felt pretty damn good.

"Chase, I don't know what to say. You're usually in trouble when you come in here and you always act like a horse's ass, but this time . . . ." The hand came away from my shoulder. "All that happened was some neighbor took the kid for a walk and you went to pieces."

"But I was responsible . . . ."

"Yes, and God knows how you'll act when you have a child of your own." He passed me another Kleenex. "What's your status with the Rivers boy?"

"What?" I wiped my face. "What . . . what are you talking about?" My tears stopped.

"Chad Rivers—that rich kid you've been dating?"

"He wants us to go to counseling," I blurted out. In my defense I can only say I was pretty upset.

"Counseling?"

I stared at the floor, shoulders slumped, feeling completely and utterly defeated. "Chad's got a problem . . . with my attitude."

"Don't we all." Warden stood up, bringing along my fanny pack. "I'll take you home. You're in no shape to drive."

I let him take me by the arm and usher me out the door. As we walked through the squad room, cops stopped what they were doing and stared. For Susan Chase to be in tears, a school bus must've been piled into by a cement truck. Truth was, a little girl had disappeared and only for a few minutes.

"Let me stop by the ladies' room. I don't want people to see me like this."

Warden nodded, then snatched the velcroed piece off the side of the pack so the Smith & Wesson tumbled into his hand. Only then did he hand me the fanny pack and point me in the direction of the john.

Outside the law enforcement center we got into one of those nondescript sedans every government official drives. Warden pulled out of the parking lot, looked both ways, and then drove north. My place was in the opposite direction.

"I thought you were taking me home."

"Changed my mind while you were in the ladies' room. We're going somewhere where we can have a talk. Once you've calmed down, I'll drop you at your jeep and you can drive home."

"I'd rather check on Megan."

"After we have our little talk."

"I'm not sure I'll be able to concentrate."

He glanced at me.

"I'm worried about Megan, J.D."

"Then call. But we are going to have this little talk."

To have our little talk Warden took me to an out-of-the-way place along Kings Highway. The atmosphere was dark and subdued. A small band played in the rear. The band was improvising as it went along, and while that's great for listening, you can't dance when you don't know where the next beat's coming from. At the moment it sounded like a variation of Ray Charles' "Georgia on My Mind." Still, there were several couples on the dance floor trying to keep time to the music.

The place must've been a former retail outlet because it was long, deep, and dark. The bar was near the door and you couldn't hear the TVs unless you sat near them. Tables and chairs were scattered between the bar on one side of the room and a long line of booths against the opposite wall. Over those booths were pictures of jazz legends, many of the pictures signed.

"Johnny!" shouted the bartender, as we came through the door. "Long time, no see."

The bartender was a white guy with some kind of accent. These days we get all kinds along the Grand Strand, and they don't always come from the Rust Belt.

"Two beers," said Warden, putting his hand in the small of my back and directing me over to a booth.

"Two?" asked the bartender.

"Two," Warden said without turning around.

I tried to take the seat where I could watch the front door, but Warden gestured me to the other side of the booth. By the time we had made ourselves comfortable, a waitress was at the booth with our beers. She was a bleached blonde wearing a black blouse and slacks. On her feet were a pair of gold shoes, and they matched the gold chain around her neck and the belt around her waist.

"Need some ID, honey," she said, clunking the mugs to the table.

"She's of age," said Warden from the other side of the booth.

"Sorry, Johnny," said the blonde, "but orders are orders."

I fished my driver's license from my fanny pack and gave it up. The woman glanced at the date, compared the picture to me, and nodded.

"It could be false," I said, some of the old Susan Chase returning.

"Sorry, honey, but that's Johnny's job, not mine."

After a long pull on my beer, I asked, "Johnny?"

"To my friends," he said flatly.

"Okay, Johnny, since we're here, we must be buds. What can I say? I lost it. I don't know what came over me. I just fucking lost it."

He pulled the Smith & Wesson out of his pocket and slid it across the table. "A great recommendation for carrying one of these."

I took the gun and slid it into the fanny pack, velcroing it in place. "Then why are you returning it?"

"Because you and I are going to have a little talk, and while you and I are having this talk, anytime you feel the need to leave, remember what I did for you tonight."

"I still might leave."

"I don't think so. You've got this convoluted sense of honor, some code you live by. You'll either return the pistol, get up, and walk home, or you'll sit there and take it."

"I still need to make my phone call."

"Use your cell phone."

"Er—I don't think it's pumped up."

"Why am I not surprised?"

As I made my way to the wall phone, the quartet broke into a Big Band number I remembered from a collaboration between Linda Ronstadt and Nelson Riddle. I reached Babe Parnell at Donna's and learned Megan was okay. If I wasn't returning soon, Babe would like to take Megan over to her place.

Figuring the idiot would do it anyway, I said, "Thanks, Babe. I'm sorry I blew up at you. I don't usually act that way." Jeez, this was pushing the envelope of bogusness.

"Oh," cooed the voice on the other end of the line, "that's all right. Everyone gets upset every once in a while. I might've done something to set you off. Are you still with the police?"

"I'm having a beer with Lieutenant Warden."

"I didn't know you knew the cops that well."

"Well," I said with a forced laugh, "I sure as hell didn't know the ones that took me downtown."

When I returned to the booth, Warden was keeping time to the music by tapping his fingers on the table. His beer stood at the same level as before I'd left.

"Sit here and take what?" I asked, sitting down.

His fingers stopped tapping. "Chase, I've never seen you break down, unless you were injured. And here you were, uninjured and slobbering all over my desk."

"I didn't slobber on your frigging desk."

"Chase, shut up and listen. I have something to say and it's about time you heard it."

Reaching for my fanny pack, I said, "If it's the same old garbage about me going back to school and getting a regular job—"

"It's not, so don't even think of returning that pistol." He placed his arms on the table and leaned forward. "You're not hitting on all cylinders. There's something wrong with you."

"I seem to have done quite well . . . so far."

"And so far it is." His beer was forgotten as he preached at me. I really didn't think Warden drank but attended a twelve-step program. "You've reached your limit. It's time to turn in your badge."

"Would you mind telling me what in the hell you're talking about?" I could see he was freaking serious.

"I'm talking about you. You can't cut it and it's best you turn in your investigative license before you get someone hurt, if not yourself."

To that I didn't know what to say.

"We don't need people on the force who break down and cry."

"I'm not on your fucking force." Forgotten was my beer now.

"But you act like it, don't you? You've gone well beyond supplementing your income as a lifeguard. And I supported your efforts in this area—"

"Because it frees up fucking man-hours for you and other departments."

"I'm not going to sit here and listen to your foul mouth."

"Well, you could leave and then you'd be rid of me and my foul mouth."

"I could just as well cuff you and return you to the law enforcement center. And you're right, searching for runaways frees up man-hours for real police work. That's why I supported you. But you've crossed the line one too many times and it's had nothing to do with tracking runaways."

"I was only following up cases the cops didn't give a . . . didn't think were important."

"Cases the police department would have gotten around to sooner or later."

"Breaking up a white slavery ring? Finding missing women? I don't think so."

"I really don't care what you think. You have no discipline and you have no desire to develop any, so you don't have a clue as to what any police department might do or might not do regarding those cases."

"And solved."

"I didn't come here to argue the merits of your accomplishments. You've killed before, and if what the State Department says is to be believed, you've even upset foreign governments."

"Yes," I said, leaning back in my side of the booth, "quite an accomplishment for a gal my age."

"Killing people?"

"You know that's not what I meant."

"In my twenty-five years of service, I've seen people come and go, and believe me, you're one who needs to go."

"Go? Like in quit?" I felt myself frown. "You're serious?"

"Yes."

"How the fuck . . . ?" I took a breath and let it out. "What do you base your evaluation on, if I might be so bold as to ask?"

"Female officers who break down don't stay on the street. Tension tears are okay, but you can't do your job if you're bawling."

"Then what do you do with them, fire them?"

"We don't spend all that money for them to wash out. If they make it through the academy, we find other assignments. Every police force does it. You don't want to lose conscientious people. There aren't enough to go around. Face it, Chase, you want to be a cop, but for you it's not going to happen. You don't have what it takes."

Now I remembered my beer. I had the urge to throw it in his face.

"Waving a pistol around in an apartment complex. The last officer who did that was off-duty, doing security work, and he was brought up on charges. You don't think your license couldn't be lifted?"

"You wouldn't dare. You people need me."

He leaned forward again. "I'll do it if you don't straighten up and fly right."

I returned the favor by jutting out my jaw. "I've been responsible for myself ever since turning fifteen and—"

"Despite everything people such as Harry Poinsett, Mickey DeShields, and I have done for you, you won't stop and take a good look at yourself. You know, people like Harry Poinsett wouldn't have the time of day for most kids your age."

"Yeah. I must really be special."

"You've got an attitude, but you also have potential. You're gifted, but you won't take direction, so you'll always have permanent potential."

"In your opinion." Warden hadn't taken a sip of his beer. He was a damn alcoholic. I knew it. I just knew it.

"Do you really think a lifeguard has an opinion anyone cares to hear?"

"I think my generation, like yours, has a right to do what it wants."

"Don't give me that generational crap. Think about what you're throwing away. Think about Chad Rivers. Or is that what this was all about?"

"Now, I truly don't know what in the hell you are talking about."

"I mean, if you mess up good enough, perhaps the Rivers family won't have anything to do with you. And maybe, just maybe, they'll be able to convince their son he's making a big mistake by marrying you."

"I'm not planning on getting married. Besides, Chad knows what I do for a living and why it's important to me."

"He does, does he? And what would he think of what you did tonight?"

"He'd think I got jazzed up over losing Megan."

"And why did you lose it when a baby was involved? What was different?"

"I was the one responsible!"

People at the table nearest us turned and stared. Behind me the band played on, lightly.

Warden lowered his voice. "That's my point. Something sent you over the edge and it's time you take a long, hard look at what this means. You and Rivers have your first child and the kid disappears, if only for a moment, will you pick up a pistol and go looking for it?"

"I just might."

"Wrong answer."

"It's my answer."

Warden glanced at his watch. "That's not what normal people do."

"It'd be my kid. Besides, I'm not having children anytime

soon. Like I said, I'm not getting married."

"And like I said, maybe that's what this is all about."

"Frigging armchair psychologist. What do you know?"

"I know that you're licensed to carry a firearm in the state of South Carolina and you were around a group of people when you went haywire. What do you think this is all about? It's about the incident tonight. It has nothing to do with you and me."

"I noticed you haven't taken a drink of your beer."

Warden glanced at the beer in front of him. "Chad Rivers hardly ever drinks. He doesn't smoke, and the only place he speeds is on the ocean, well away from shore."

"I don't own a boat like his."

Warden shook his head. "An answer for every question. Really, when are you going to act your age?"

"I'm a young person. I'm supposed to have a good time, and your job, as an old fart, is to try to make me do otherwise."

He stared at me as I drank deeply from my beer. Behind me the band broke into something that made me want to dance. Several couples wove their way through tables and chairs to a small, wooden dance floor. I wished Chad and his broad shoulders were here. We could dance and dance, and turn this night around.

And he was. At our booth. Jeans, collarless shirt, and a windbreaker that didn't protect his hair from the wind. It was a mess again.

I was startled. "What are you doing here?"

"Wondering if you'd like to dance," he said with that easy smile that turns me to jelly.

Looking at Warden, I said, "You called him."

"All sorts of people come in here." Warden pushed his beer across the table as he slid out of the booth. "Take this, Chase, even if you won't take my advice."

I'm proud to say I thanked him for the beer, then got to my feet and danced to the funny music with my Main Man.

Old people can be such a drag. If Chad and I ever did get married and I did start punching out kids, I wouldn't turn into someone like J.D. Warden. No. It appeared I would turn into another kind of monster.

4

The night Donna died and Megan disappeared was during a winter storm that swept ashore drenching everything with a freezing rain and overwhelming the drainage
system. To compound things, the tide was in. Water was
everywhere, sometimes as much as half a foot on the high-
ways. And while the Grand Strand knew the storm was on
its way, we were told it would move inland. Wrong. It stalled
over the beach. For nearly six hours we received a soaking
that seemed like it would go on forever. Donna and Megan
weren't the only casualties.

An old lady who prided herself on going to the mailbox
every day, rain or shine, evidently lost her footing and was
washed down the curb to the corner, where a UPS truck,
unable to see anything in the downpour, ran over her legs.
These days the old lady uses a wheelchair to check her mail.
A child, coming home from school and playing in the gut-
ters, stepped into a hole with his pack on his back and was
washed into the sewer. Horrified, his friends could only watch
as the boy was sucked into a drainage pool, where, weighted
down by his backpack, he floundered and drowned.

Two men, golfing in slickers and waders, overturned their

cart when they tried to cross one of the concrete gullies built to carry away excess water. When the cart flipped, one of the men fell out and was swept into a culvert, where his body was later found with other flotsam jammed against a huge metal grate. The medical examiner said the man had died when the cart overturned because there was no water in his lungs. This was revealed in the lawsuit the man's widow brought against the golf course for allowing her husband to take to the links that day. His partner, the one who'd held onto the cart until he was rescued, was heard to remark it was a damn shame: the dead man had been ahead by more than four strokes at the turn.

It appears that Donna was driving home when her VW hydroplaned across the bypass. What the hell she was doing out in this weather with the baby I have no idea. No one saw the accident. The rain was blowing in off the ocean and hitting cars at the perpendicular. The car was discovered the following morning by a man looking for a skiff. The rear bumper was all that could be seen—Donna's car lay in a pool of water—and by noon a wrecker was at the site, pulling it to the roadbed. No one had reported the vehicle missing. To the cops that meant the vehicle was either stolen or worse. It was worse.

By then a crowd had gathered and there was a hush as the car was dragged from the water. The winch operator could see nothing, but when he went forward, he saw the body of a young woman lying across the front seat. The window on the passenger side was busted out and the baby seat empty.

Warden brought me the news. He also brought along Harry Poinsett. At the door of the cabin of my family's former shrimp boat, I brushed back my hair and asked, "What's this—another storm party?" I wore jeans and a sweatshirt and not much of anything else. "You're too late. That was last night."

To open the door I had to kick a gin bottle out of the way. It clunked into the far bulkhead. Chad and I had been trapped in here all night—to my delight. Nothing like a raging storm to bring out the squealer in me. Early this morning my sweet man had dragged himself out of bed and headed off to work, complaining that his 'vette had been nicked by one of the pines uprooted by the storm.

When neither Harry nor Warden smiled, I asked, "What?" A tremor ran through me. "Chad? What happened?"

Warden shook his head, so did Dads. "He's on his way over."

"On his way over? What then?" I wanted to snatch J.D. by his highly starched shirt and beat the info out of him. "What, for God's sake? Tell me!"

"It's Donna Destefani."

"What about her?"

"Can we come in, Susan?" asked Dads.

I nodded, then backed out of their way. The room was a mess, but I didn't notice, as if I ever do.

Warden followed Harry into the living quarters of the shrimp boat. Harry took my arm and ushered me over to the broken-down sofa. After sitting down, Dads continued to hold my hand.

"How'd it happen?"

"In the storm," said Warden, taking some clothes off a rocker and tossing them out of the way. Warden glanced around the pilothouse, which had been expanded to give me room for a couple of bunk beds and a gas stove.

"Where?" I could barely ask.

"On the bypass."

"Where?" I asked again, my voice going hoarse.

The location was to the north of us, nowhere near where Donna lived or worked.

"What was she doing there?"

Warden shrugged.

"And Megan?"

Warden looked at the floor.

It was then that I lost it.

When I came to my senses I went searching for my god-child, and nothing said by Chad, Dads, Warden, or Mickey Dee could discourage me. I canvassed the creek where the VW had been found, laying out grids and covering every inch. I was properly motivated. Visions of what a baby would look like if an animal got hold of her flashed through my head. I forced the images away and pushed through the underbrush. When I found any piece of trash, any little shred of hope, sometimes I yelped; sometimes I burst into tears over the least little thing, like a river snake or an ocean crab. Those yelps brought Chad and Dads running. Soon Harry had all he could take and wouldn't go out again. He was replaced by Mickey DeShields.

Chad was always there, and once or twice his mother stopped by. Lois stood by the edge of the road and watched me fight my way through the underbrush and the suck-you-down muck. I'd taken to carrying a machete, and because of the way I swung it, no one dared come near me, even the priest from St. Michael's. That was okay by me. I was going to find my godchild if it was the last thing I did.

Babe Parnell wouldn't search at all. She said both Donna and Megan were dead and it was time to let them go. Each day she came to the search area and delivered the same message. Sometimes she brought along the priest. My response was ugly, sometimes not even that nice. The evening of the third day, Babe stopped by my boat. Her eyes were puffy and her makeup unevenly applied. She ignored the messy quarters and took a seat in the rocker. By then, Max the Wonder Dog, my brown Lab, had taken up residence with Harry, and who could blame the animal.

I hadn't moved from the sofa once I'd collapsed onto it after another long day in the swamp. My clothes were nasty. I stunk and shivered from a long day in the muck. The beat-up coffee table was littered with dirty glasses, empty soda cans, and half-eaten meals. I'd pulled a bottle of gin from under the bar and collapsed with it on the sofa. By now I was sucking straight from the bottle.

In contrast, Babe was handsomely dressed and sober. She unbuttoned the knee-length coat when she sat down. Under it she wore a plain white blouse with no jewelry and a navy blue skirt. On her feet were a pair of boots, fur sticking out the top.

She cleared her throat. "The funeral's tomorrow."

I didn't say anything. For all I cared the woman could be talking to herself.

"While you were searching for Megan, I made all the arrangements. Her mother and father-in-law will drive up from Charleston, but I don't know if Mrs. Destefani will understand what's going on. She's pretty well gone and her husband has his hands full. He sounded relieved that all the arrangements had been made. Donna and Megan will be buried in Socastee, not far from here, so you can visit the gravesite."

"Megan . . . buried?"

"Yes, we have to let her go. You have to let her go."

"But there's no body."

"Susan, Megan will be put to rest, if not by you, by everyone else."

I lay on the sofa and watched Babe take a handkerchief from her purse and dab at her eyes.

"I had movers come in and pack up everything, the furniture, the clothes. Robert's parents don't have any use for anything but a few mementos and pictures I left on the kitchen counter. The rest goes to Goodwill. I felt just awful, going through her things. But what could I do?"

"There's no hurry . . . ."

"Yes, there is. I'm leaving the Grand Strand. The resident manager gave me a break on my rent and I'm moving on."

"Moving on?"

"I—I can't stand it. You might be able to live here and never think of Donna and Megan—"

"I think of them all the fucking time."

48

The woman's chin trembled. "I didn't mean . . . it's just that things haven't worked out for me once again."

"I know what you mean." I took another long pull from the bottle. Chad was pissed about all my drinking and Dads was keeping his distance.

She scanned the crowded cabin, its only bright spot the painting over the couch by Jenny Rogers, another lost soul. "I really thought it was going to work out, but it didn't. I'm glad you understand. Most people don't." She stood.

"But why tell me?"

"Donna thought so highly of you . . . I didn't know who else . . . ." She pulled a set of keys from her purse and held them out where I could see them. "One of the keys is to the car in the county compound, the other is to the apartment."

"Leave them on the table."

She nodded, jerkily, then put the keys on the coffee table among the clutter. "Thank you, Susan."

As she headed for the door, I asked, "How'd you find me?" When people think of the Grand Strand they don't think of the Waterway.

"I had to call others about the funeral, and one of them told me your boat was permanently moored at Wacca Wache Landing. I didn't know where that was." She smiled. "But I found it."

"You could've called. You didn't have to come all the way out here."

"I had to tell you face-to-face." When I said nothing, she pulled the heavy coat around her and turned for the door.

"Thanks, Babe."

The woman flashed a nervous smile. "Out of all the people I've met, I knew you'd understand."

But I didn't understand. Not for several days, then I got the signal loud and clear. Not that it did me any good. I couldn't find anyone who'd believe me.

My boyfriend arrived the morning of the funeral and let

49

himself in with his key. I slept on the couch with the phone off, and damn if he didn't throw water in my face. I thought that was only done in the movies. Evidently not.

"What—what?" I came up fighting—until my head rang with pain. "Oh, God."

Chad was dressed in sweats, but his hair looked orderly enough to go out on a date. Over the back of the rocking chair hung his business suit, white shirt, and rep tie.

"It's time to get ready for the funeral."

I wiped the water off and lay back down. Jeez, my head was killing me. "I'm not going."

"She was your friend, Suze."

"I'm still not going." Tears formed in my eyes, whether from the death of Donna or the hangover, I couldn't tell.

"You were the child's godparent."

I opened my eyes. "Did they find Megan?"

Chad shook his head.

"Then I'm not going," I said, closing my eyes and wishing the world would go away, my boyfriend included. There was a good chance I was going to be sick, and it was no fun cleaning up. That's why I stick with linoleum decks.

"You're expected to be there."

"I don't have to do shit." Opening my eyes again, I looked up. "You don't look like you're dressed for a funeral."

"I'm dressed in the event I have to dress you."

The first smile crossed my face since I had heard of the death of Donna and that Megan had gone missing. "That's a switch. Usually you're more interested in undressing me."

"And I'm going to do it," he said, stepping toward the sofa. "If you don't get up."

"I'm not going anywhere," I said, closing my eyes.

"I'm going to count to three."

"Then what?"

"I'll dump you in the shower with your clothes on. That's 'one.'"

"Listen," I said, opening my eyes and coming up on an

elbow, "I've told you I'm not going, so get over it. I don't think Donna will miss me."

"That's damn selfish of you, and that's 'two.'"

"Oh," I said, smiling again, "my good boy's going to start cursing now."

"It's to let you know I'm damn serious."

I lay back down. "Please go away. My head's killing me." I opened an eye to glance at the bar. "Unless you're going out for something to drink. I think I'm running low."

"Three. Get up, Susan."

I closed my eyes.

"This is your last warning."

With my eyes closed and a smile on my face, I said, "I love it when you're so masterful—"

My arm was nearly jerked out of its socket. My eyes flew open and the room swung around as Chad dipped his shoulder and lifted me over his back.

"Chad!"

When he settled me on his back, I squawked again. "You'd better put me down. I'm going to be sick."

"Then do it in the shower."

My head was about to explode and my stomach had begun to stir. "I'm warning you. I'm going to puke."

At the head he bent over, let me slide off his back, and stood me on my feet. Then, bracing me against the bulkhead, forearm across my chest, he kept me on my feet. Once the shower was going, he loosened his grip across my chest, probably the only reason I hadn't thrown up. My stomach was really boiling. I stayed in the stall until I finished with my toilette, which included throwing up more than once.

Babe had thought of everything, down to a small casket representing Megan. What'd happened to the baby, no one knew, and I'd lived along the coast long enough to know scavengers had gotten it even before I'd started searching. I shuddered. It was harder and harder to keep those images at bay.

On the way over to St. Michael's, I had made Chad stop by the liquor store for a bottle of vodka on the off chance it was true that you couldn't smell vodka on a person's breath. Then I staggered into the church and took my seat beside a disapproving Harry Poinsett and a smiling Babe Parnell.

Babe leaned across Dads. "I knew you'd come."

"Then you knew better than me."

"No, no, Susan, you're a survivor, just like me."

"I would've rather Donna and Megan had survived."

When the ache in my heart reached my face, I burst into tears.

The following day Dads came over and told me I had to go see Parnell before she left town.

"Why, for cripe's sake?"

Harry stared at me where I lay on the couch clutching a bottle of gin. "First," said Harry, ticking off the reasons on his fingers, "because you owe it to the woman for taking up your slack—"

"She didn't take up—"

"Susan, don't interrupt. It's rude. Besides, the ability to accept responsibility is the measure of the man."

"Then that let's me off the hook. I'm a woman."

"Two, you need to stop feeling sorry for yourself. You're not responsible for Megan's death. It was an accident. It could've happened to anyone in such a storm. Third, because if you don't put this behind you, I don't think Chad's coming back. He's never seen you drink like this before."

"Neither have I."

Dads gave me the fish eye.

A half hour later I was tooling up the bypass toward Myrtle Beach.

A workman was in Parnell's apartment, a tall, bony guy with freckles that turned out to be paint specks. He wore jeans and a tee shirt, also speckled where paint had hit them.

A mask hung around his neck, a paper thing.

"Yo!" I shouted, entering the apartment.

"Back here!"

Parnell's place was a one-bedroom and the painter was in there.

"What can I do for you, ma'am?"

"I was looking . . . ." Glancing around the empty room, I finished, "I was looking for Connie Parnell."

"She's gone."

Shit. Dads would not be pleased, and in fact I was a little tired of feeling sorry for myself.

"I was supposed to be in here two days ago, but I was held up with another job." The painter pointed at a window where you could see the beach. "They've already got this one leased. Asked for a whole year lease because it overlooks the beach. That's why I'm supposed to do it quick." He looked around. "It won't take much time. The woman don't seemed to hardly lived here."

"There was only her."

"And the baby."

"Baby?"

"There was baby food in the refrigerator."

"She used to baby-sit for a friend of mine in 202."

"Miz Destefani?" When I nodded, he said, "That's too bad. I know it's not the same, and I wouldn't want to try to make it out to be, but I lost a good hunting dog in that storm. Been four days and that dog still ain't come home. I'm afraid he was washed down some drain pipe and drowned."

It damn well wasn't the same. My godchild had disappeared, and right now this bastard's dog could be feeding on her carcass.

The room began to move.

I was on the floor, looking up at the young man. He held something in my face and it had a pungent odor. I pushed the . . . diaper away.

"Enough already!"

"Take it easy," he said, finally taking the god-awful smell away. "I'll call 911."

"No . . . need." Whew! It was good to be able to breathe—clean air, that is. "Just help me up."

He did, and I sat there, against the wall, staring at the diaper. One of Megan's left behind when Parnell had moved out.

The young man was still hunched over and his hand was on my arm as if he was afraid I might fall over. "Sorry about the diaper, but it was the only thing handy and I didn't want to leave you. You sure you're gonna be okay?"

"Donna was a friend of mine, her daughter my godchild. Catholic, lots of pomp and ceremony."

The painter said he was sorry again, meaning he didn't need any hysterical woman on his hands, especially one spouting off about the peculiarities of the Catholic church.

"I'm sorry. I'm babbling. Help me to my feet."

"Ma'am," he said, with a hand firmly on my shoulder. "How about waiting a couple of minutes. It'd make me feel a lot better, even if it doesn't you."

When I did as he said, he disappeared into the kitchen and then returned. "I've got to check to see if anything was left up in the crawl space. You be okay?"

I nodded, then sat there as he rustled around in the closet. I was taking her death way too seriously, but every time I told myself that hundreds of babies died each day, I'd break down and cry. Tears welled up again and I quickly blotted them with the collar of my blouse.

The painter stepped out of the closet. "Really not much to do, but the place will get the full treatment. Thought there was something in that hole in the ceiling, but whatever she stored up there's gone. Always seems to be a waste of good money for a whole apartment to be repainted when you have a person who walked on egg shells." He grinned. "But I'll take the money anytime."

"Walked on . . . egg shells?"

He came over and squatted down in front of me. "The bathroom's cleaner than what's normal for a single gal and there's not a mark on the walls where she might've bumped into it with a piece of furniture. No pictures hung, no stains on the carpet, no nothing. It was like she was never here."

I could see what he meant. The empty bedroom had been recently vacuumed and the molding wiped down.

"Surprising she'd leave her trash behind. Neatniks never leave nothing behind." He pulled me to my feet. "I've cleaned up behind them before. They think you can tell their family secrets by the stuff left behind."

Trying my legs, I walked into the kitchen. "When did you say you were supposed to paint this place?"

"Two days ago."

"That was the day of the funeral."

He looked at me blankly.

I picked up the diaper from the counter and unwrapped the plastic square. It was full of fresh baby shit. When I stuck my finger into the mess, the young man made a face.

"Ma'am, did you hurt your head when you hit the floor?"

"It's been a week since Megan disappeared . . . ." I said more to myself than to him. "And yet there's this fresh diaper." I opened the refrigerator door. Two used bottles of baby food sat there.

"I've got to get started on this unit. If I can have it finished by tonight, they can move in tomorrow."

"You might have a problem. SLED will want to check this out."

As usual my cell phone was dead, but the painter's worked just fine. Connected with Lt. Warden, I said, "Come out to Parnell's apartment. You've got a problem."

"Chase, are you in trouble with the uniformed division again?"

"It's not me, it's—"

"Evidently you didn't hear anything I said last week."

"J.D.!"

"Take it up with the uniforms. They can bring you downtown and we'll talk. This time in a holding cell."

"You want me to call the FBI?"

"Now why would you do that?" But I had his attention. The *feebs* loved to lord it over the locals.

"There's been a kidnapping."

Warden arrived the same time as the uniforms, who had been called, once again, by the apartment manager. The heavy woman wore the same robe and her hair was still up in rollers. Warden got rid of the uniforms.

The painter gestured at me sitting on the counter top and smoking a cigarette. He said, "This young lady's in the way of my work."

"Mine too," grumbled Warden.

I cut them off with, "Megan Destefani is still alive. She didn't die in the storm."

"Chase, you know there's a limit to what people will take before they file a complaint."

"That's right," said the manager from the door. The heavy woman was taking no chances. She did not come inside.

"This is the second time I've bailed you out in the last two weeks."

"I'm not worried about your reputation but my godchild."

"The baby who drowned?"

"She didn't drown," I said, tossing him the used diaper.

He fielded the thing and opened it. I could tell by the way his nose twisted up that he got the message. "What's this all about?"

"She fell down and hit her head," said the painter. "She's been out of her head ever since she come to."

Warden stared at me. "You fell down?"

"I was a little dizzy. That's all."

"Maybe you need to see a doctor."

"It's the diaper, J.D. Megan was supposed to have disappeared a week ago."

"So?"

"Has it been so long since you've changed a diaper that you've forgotten this shit's supposed to dry? At least in a week." Gesturing at the empty food bottles, I added, "And there's this."

He glanced at the baby food bottles. The food in the empty bottles had dried, and I recognized them as the kind of food Megan liked.

"The diaper was where?"

"Ask him," I said, gesturing at the painter. "He found it."

"It was on the counter." He pointed at me. "Right where she's sitting."

"And wrapped into a tight little bundle, with this piece of tape?" he asked, pointing to the tabs securing the diaper.

"Er—yes."

"Chase, what do you think you have? I don't have a lot of time for foolishness."

"Neither do I," injected the painter.

"Megan's body wasn't found and now I know why."

"Why?"

"Because she was hidden here, maybe in the crawl space, and fed something that would keep her quiet." Looking at the resident manager, I asked, "Parnell asked for the top floor, didn't she?"

The manager shrugged in her tent dress and it did appear that mountains could move. "Lots of folks ask for the top floor. They want to be away from the noise. I tell them there ain't no noise in this place. Not by our residents anyway."

I ignored the crack. "When Parnell realized Donna was dead and the child thought to be missing, she decided to have a baby of her own, without all the fuss."

"You're suggesting Parnell stole the child?"

"She's loony."

"That's the pot calling the kettle black," said the painter. "Hey, I really need to get started here."

To Warden's credit, he asked the guy to wait in the hall until he finished interviewing me.

After the painter had gone, I said, "Parnell left town after the funeral. Right after taking care of all the details that would bury Megan Destefani and any questions with her." I swallowed. "Including a visit to the child's godparent. Constance Delphine Parnell stole Donna Destefani's baby."

Warden shook his head. "Sounds like another one of your crazy theories."

I slipped off the counter and put out my cigarette in the sink. "What're you saying, that you're not going to look for Megan?"

"I don't have proof she's even missing."

"The diaper—"

"Means what? I suppose we could find the same evidence if we searched Destefani's apartment, too."

"Because that's her home!"

"And this is the home of her baby-sitter. So it stands to reason there would be dirty diapers here."

"Not one a few days old. Don't you see, Megan was here, just a couple of days ago."

"You have no proof of that."

I gestured at the diaper.

"What am I supposed to do, run a lab test on this . . . shit?"

I had to smile. It was the first time I'd ever heard Warden use such language. "That'd be a start. Megan has grandparents who'd like to have their granddaughter returned."

"And I suppose you're going to run right over and upset them?"

"I'm sure as hell not going to let that Parnell woman get away with kidnapping."

He shook his head. "I don't know . . . ."

My hands went to my hips. "Then I'll find Megan myself, and I'll start by interviewing everyone who was in the complex the night of the storm."

"You'll be lucky if you find anyone who wasn't at home the night of that storm. That doesn't mean they will've seen Parnell with a baby."

The painter returned. "Am I going to be able to get in here today? I got a living to make."

Warden stared at me, then said, "Not today."

"But this ain't right. I heard you two arguing. You got no reason to keep me out of here."

"He's right," said the resident manager, putting in her two tons' worth. "We've got a deadline to meet."

"Tell him, J.D."

Warden ground his teeth before flashing his shield. "I'm from the State Law Enforcement Division and you're contaminating a potential crime scene by remaining here."

"Crime scene?"

"He's got to dust for prints," I explained. "He'll need yours, so don't go far." To the fat woman, I said, "Yours, too."

"Chase, don't push it. I'm only taking prints so if, and I say 'if,' the child has been abducted, we'll have usable prints for an investigation."

But they didn't find any, not even those prints left on the backside of doorknobs or under drawers where criminals always forget to wipe. Not a single print, except the painter's and mine. It was just as I thought. Babe Parnell was on the run from someone, and now that someone was me.

5

I was packing the footlocker mounted in the rear of my jeep when Chad pulled into the parking lot of the landing. As Chad stepped out of his Corvette, I noticed he was wearing a pair of dark corduroy pants, half boots, and a flannel shirt under an open windbreaker. His brown hair was being teased by the wind and there was a serious look on his face.

It was cold. But not as cold as where Donna Destefani lay, and that was what I assumed Chad was here to talk about. During the last couple of days, while installing a pizza satellite dish on Dads' schooner, Harry and I had had several long talks about Donna and Megan, and what I was about to do. I assumed Chad was here to put the final nail in the coffin of my speculations.

I didn't want to fight. Truth was, I was still embarrassed at how he'd had to brace me about the funeral. Finding something inside the footlocker to rearrange, I stayed hunched over the metal box, only my ass sticking out the door of the jeep.

A pair of feet crunched to a stop on the parking lot gravel. "You didn't tell me you were leaving."

Keeping my nose firmly stuck in the locker, I said, "I'll

only be gone for a day or two."

"And you didn't want me to come along?"

My head came up, almost hitting the roll bar. "I—I didn't think you could get away. You know, with your Dad building the new boat."

"Here I am." He smiled that smile that made my stomach hollow with excitement. "I have a bag in the car. Want me to get it?"

"Sure . . . *sure!*" I was still gaping at him when he returned.

There was plenty of room in the footlocker. I don't pack all the usual girl stuff. If you're only going to see someone once, like the person you're questioning, why bring along more than a couple of outfits?

"Harry thought you should have some company. Don't you think he's being a little too overprotective?"

All I could do was nod in agreement and fall even more in love with this guy. Maybe it was time to put my biker chick days behind me.

Chad went around to the passenger side and opened the door. "Are we good to go?"

"Er—I really hadn't finished packing." I ran back to *Daddy's Girl* and quickly dug out a few more outfits.

A half hour later we were tooling up Kings Highway. Chad was in the passenger seat and I was driving.

"What've you learned about this Parnell woman?" Chad had to raise his voice over the wind whistling through the sides of the jeep.

"Babe left town without asking for her security deposit to be returned."

"Could have been upset over the death of her friend and the friend's daughter?"

I glanced at him.

"Just playing devil's advocate."

"I'm not sure I'm going to like this as much as I thought.

It's like having Dads tagging along."

"Really," said Chad, slipping a hand between my legs, then running it up between my thighs.

I gasped and had trouble controlling the jeep. Someone blew a horn. Crazy kids, you could hear them yelling. Don't even concentrate on their driving.

The hand came out of my crotch. "Sorry, Suze, but you shouldn't be comparing me to Harry Poinsett."

"Don't worry," I said breathlessly. "I won't make that mistake again. Um-m—want to drive?"

"No, no." He smiled. "I'd rather sit here and daydream."

"Think we'll need to stop before reaching North Carolina?"

He laughed. "I think you need to tell me what you've learned about this Parnell woman."

"Like I said, she left her security deposit behind."

"They could be mailing it to her."

I glanced at him again. "You do know the right questions to ask, don't you?"

"McMillan and boyfriend, I presume."

"This might be fun, having you along."

"It took you this long to figure that out?"

"Santee Cooper owes Parnell forty-two seventy-six on her security deposit for her power bill. But to answer your questions, Connie Parnell left no forwarding address. Warden blew that off for the same reason—the distraught neighbor."

"I'm not so sure he blew anything off. I doubt you were able to learn all this as a private eye."

He was right about that.

"The previous address Parnell gave when she moved into the Pirate's Cove," asked Chad, "you know, when they ask where you've lived the last five years?"

"Bogus."

"So the woman's paranoid."

"Which, on the face of it, is not a problem—"

"But you have a problem with it."

"I've got a real problem with losing Megan. That's why

we're headed to Waxhaw. I want to find out if Constance Delphine Parnell is real or not."

"You have no other leads?"

"It's the only place she called home. The rest was about the Alamo, Wyatt Earp, and the Lost Colony. Parnell's a history buff. Said she made money writing articles for magazines, but I couldn't find anything in the library under her name for the last five years. It was the same on the Internet."

"Maybe she uses a pen name."

"For nonfiction?"

"Okay. Then let's check *The Lost Colony*. It's just up the road."

"It's closed this time of year. No Babe Parnell or Constance Delphine Parnell is working there, nor anyone matching her description."

"Jiminy, Susan. Did you check out the Alamo and the Tombstone Territory, too?"

"The Alamo didn't have anyone matching Babe's description, nor does anyone in the local historical society know her. The same goes for Tombstone."

Except for the wind whistling through the sides of the jeep the vehicle went silent.

I saw Chad staring at me. "What? What?"

"I'm either impressed with the thoroughness of your investigation or I agree with Warden that you have some major jones for this woman."

Taking 501 inland, we drove past where the Rivers family builds their boats. Chad stared out the plastic window and looked at the boatyard. "I can't understand why any woman would steal another woman's baby. It's sick." He faced the windshield again. "I think Megan was lost during the storm— if you want my opinion."

"Donna always buckled her in."

"She wasn't buckled in herself."

"How did you know?"

"I asked Lieutenant Warden."

We drove along in silence. In a few minutes, I said, "Look, I really appreciate your coming along."

"No problem."

"I didn't call you and tell you I was going because I thought you'd be mad."

"Mad? Yes, I think you're quite mad, Suze, but I'm not mad at you."

"It could be fun, going out of town together."

"Oh, yes," he said with a laugh. "My idea of an overnighter with the girl I love: tracking down an apparition. Where is it you said we're headed?"

"Waxhaw, North Carolina."

"The birthplace of Andrew Jackson?"

"How'd you know?"

"One of the hazards of a higher education." He shifted around in his seat. "So how do you go about investigating someone?"

"You follow leads. If you don't have a lead, you have to come up with one. Talking with people will usually give you something to follow up."

"With a name like 'Constance Delphine Parnell' and the nickname 'Babe,' you shouldn't have any trouble. What she does for a living—is that a possible trace?"

"Babe loved history and turned it into her vocation, writing articles for magazines, historical fillers, and such."

"Fillers?"

"That stuff at the bottom of a page when an article's too short to fill a page of a magazine."

"You can make a living doing that?"

"If you love what you do, you get by."

He looked at me sharply. "Are we going to fight all the way to Waxhaw?"

"When it comes to the guy I love, I want him to know there are subjects I'm serious about. I don't think I could marry a man who doesn't enjoy his work."

"I like building boats."

"So who's going to run the company?"

"I haven't figured that out yet."

"Your mother should've had more children."

"It always gets around to my mother."

To that I said nothing.

"I know I have a problem with my mom, but I don't think it helps ticking her off."

"Leave that to me."

"Susan, Susan, I don't know about you . . . ."

I took his hand and gave it a squeeze. "Well, I know about you, my man. You're one hell of a guy, Chad Rivers, and I don't want to lose you."

"You still might, if you're wrong about Parnell."

My hand slipped away from his. In the back of my mind was his threat the day we had argued at Donna's, that he was tough enough to walk away from me.

"Warden thinks Megan's body will turn up. His partner, that black man?"

"Mickey DeShields."

"DeShields seems to understand the body will never be found, or if it is, it won't be recognizable. This isn't some piece of farm land or inner city. This is the Carolina coast and our weather, not to mention the creatures—"

I shivered. "Could we change the subject?" Megan had to be alive. She just had to be, and with Babe Parnell. I wouldn't consider the alternative. I couldn't consider the alternative.

"I wanted to see what you do. I talked it over with my dad. He thought it was a good idea. Mother agreed."

I glanced at him. "She did?"

"She did."

"Then what's bothering you?"

"I agree with Harry Poinsett that you have a problem with closure when it comes to your godchild."

"More armchair psychology."

"Yes, Suze," he said with a warm smile, "but you have to admit you make a fascinating case study."

We took US 76 almost into Florence, then caught I-20 heading west toward Columbia and turned north at Camden on 601.

Camden is where Andrew Jackson and his brother were held during the Revolutionary War. The state of South Carolina had more battles fought inside its borders than any of the other thirteen colonies. Knowing stuff like that is one of the hazards of mooring your boat beside a senior citizen. But I'm proud to say I've never stopped and read a roadside marker.

Until his capture in April 1781, Andy, only thirteen, was serving as an orderly and messenger when a British raiding party captured his unit. Sometime during his incarceration the British commander wanted his boots cleaned and ordered young Andy to scrub them. The thirteen-year-old refused, arguing he had rights as a POW, that he wasn't some bootlicker. The officer lashed out at him with his sword and Andrew threw up a hand to protect himself. The blade slashed Andy's hand to the bone and left a cut across his head, scars that Jackson carried for the rest of his life. It goes without saying that I have a great deal of admiration for young Andrew Jackson.

Waxhaw, North Carolina, is a town of fewer than two thousand, and the people living there have made a determined effort to avoid the effects of the latter half of the twentieth century. Waxhaw, however, is only a half hour's drive from Charlotte, and its suburban sprawl and strip malls have overflowed into Union County. Filled with disdain for the Queen City, Waxhaw has kept its single-traffic-light downtown alive by attracting antique and consignment shops.

A quick check of the current phone book turned up no one by the name of Constance Delphine Parnell. While still at the beach, I'd used the Internet's phone book to get maps to all the Parnell addresses, but tracing those would take lots of legwork. Instead, I went to the police department and sent Chad browsing.

"But I want to help," he protested.

"And help you will, but I can't make this happen with you tagging along."

"Maybe I shouldn't've come along at all."

"Hey, no pouting or I'll dump your pretty little ass somewhere along the road."

"I was hoping you might need me."

"I will. Tonight."

"Just a sex object, am I?" But he smiled before climbing out of the jeep and wandering down the street.

The Waxhaw chief of police sat behind a wooden desk with little paperwork in front of him. His office was open and empty. A door led to the cell block. There wasn't a dispatcher, only a radio and mike on a table along one of the walls and another desk, probably for another cop. Town this size couldn't have more than two. The nameplate said: "Roy Scruggs."

"Looking for directions?" he asked with a smile.

I took a seat and opened my coat. Underneath it I wore a white blouse and gray slacks with a wide belt. I wanted to look business-like but girlish and didn't want to freeze my ass off. "How'd you know?"

"Because that's what most folks come in here for." He pushed his paperwork aside and picked up a legal pad. This man was serious about giving directions.

"Name's Chase. Susan Chase, from Myrtle Beach."

That's where I usually stop and let them get in a word edgewise. Most have some sort of feelings about the Grand Strand, good or bad, and you are a damn fool if you don't let them vent.

The chief leaned back in his chair. "Myrtle Beach. Go there

every summer. Like to fight the big ones. After a while bass fishing becomes a little too predictable." He glanced out the windows overlooking the street. "This time of year they become very particular about when and where they'll strike."

"I'm looking for a friend of mine, Constance Delphine Parnell. Called 'Babe' for short. She wasn't listed in the phone book, so that's why I came to you. Maybe you can tell me how to find her. Babe's shorter than me, similar build, and her hair is really short, dark brown. She grew up somewhere around Waxhaw. She's a couple of years older than me."

The chief scratched his head with his pen. "You don't have an address?"

"We were in school together and I lost touch when she graduated. I was on my way to Charlotte and thought I'd take a stab at finding her."

He put down the pen. "Remember anything about her family?"

I smiled. "You know kids. Parents were an intrusion. Unless they sent money."

"Well, I've been chief of police for the last twenty years and I probably know more than I care to about the teenagers in Union County. Union County is the county you're in, but my jurisdiction is only for the town. The new elementary school is in my jurisdiction, but for a fender-bender in their parking lot you'd have to call the county sheriff."

Did I really need to know this? Or was this guy thinking while his mouth ran on autopilot. "Then you don't remember her?"

"I don't think I ever knew any Babe Parnell."

"That's odd. Babe was a real student of history. She knew everything about Waxhaw. You know, where Jackson was born, all that stuff, his uncle's house being across the road, and the road being the boundary between North and South Carolina."

"He was born in North Carolina, Miss Chase. I know what the people in South Carolina say. If I were you, I'd stop by the high school and have a talk with Martha Perkins. She knows Union County. In the county library they have a book—an awfully thin book I must admit—and that book was written by Martha Perkins. If this friend of yours was from around here, she'll be able to put you onto her, or to someone who knows her. She taught at the old high school."

"Would there be a cluster of Parnells somewhere, like the people I saw in the phone book? I thought I might knock on a few doors."

"You seem awfully interested in finding this woman."

I laughed. "Well, she does owe me a hundred and forty bucks."

"And the college you two attended?"

"Rutledge, down the road."

The chief stared at me for the longest, then opened his center desk drawer and pulled out a sheet of paper which he laid on top of the desk and turned around to face me. On the paper was an artist's rendition of Babe Parnell and a poster asking anyone having information about her where-abouts to immediately contact the South Carolina State Law Enforcement Division. Their toll-free number was at the bottom of the page.

My face burned, my ears roared, and for a moment, I couldn't hear what he was saying.

". . . be along and for me to help out anyway I could. He said you wouldn't shoot straight but would concoct some outlandish tale about why you were looking for this girl."

"Lieutenant Warden thinks I'm on a wild goose chase."

"And why's that?"

I told him about Donna's death and her daughter's dis-appearance during the winter storm.

"Knowing that, I don't think I would have bothered with an all-points bulletin. You know, Miss Chase, people like me are here to help, not obstruct you."

"I'll keep that in mind," I said, standing up.

"Sit back down. I haven't given you those directions."

Chad was still gone when I returned to the jeep. So I sat there chewing gum with the heater blasting until I saw him step out of an antique shop a couple of doors away. Although it was the dead of winter, the place was alive with tourists. They were all over the place, jaywalking across the main street, which was lined with mulch and trimmed-back shrubs. At both ends of the street where the rows of shops ended were sprawled huge parking lots where buildings had been razed to make way for tour buses. As we had driven into town, signs proclaimed Waxhaw to be "The Antique Capital of the World."

Chad slid into the jeep. "Know what I found?"

I shook my head, then popped my gum.

"A Spanish walnut bonnet chest. You know how unique that is?"

"Er—no."

"Two hundred years old, if it's a day. I've only seen them in books." He was breathless with excitement. "Imagine, Spanish walnut."

I nodded, not knowing what to say. To me furniture was simply something you kept stuff in.

"It's a dresser with a compartment on top where ladies kept their hats."

"That explains that," I said, popping my gum again. "I don't wear anything but baseball caps."

He glanced at the jail. "What'd the sheriff say?"

"He gave me a lead."

"Uh-huh." Chad wasn't looking at me or the jail. He was staring down Main Street.

"Well, are you going to buy it or not? Unless it's real small, I don't think I can get it into the jeep."

"My mother would love it."

"So get it."

Now he faced me. "I'd have to ship it home or send someone from the plant to pick it up."

I shrugged. "If it makes you happy."

"It would make my mother happy. She's always wanted one for the guest room."

"Chad, I've got to run out to the high school. You want to stay here and do some more shopping?"

A rather wistful look crossed his face as he looked down Main Street again. "I've heard my mother talk about this place. I never would've believed there could be so many antiques. I met some people from Germany. I couldn't follow everything they said, but they were excited about what they'd found. They weren't worried about the price, only how they were going to get the piece back to Berlin."

He gave me a peck on the cheek before climbing out. "I didn't know sleuthing could be so much fun. I'm going to buy that chest for my mother if they take American Express." He glanced at his watch. "Meet you here at three?"

I glanced at my watch. "Make that four. I may have to wait to see this teacher."

"Then you'll take care of your own lunch and I'll take care of mine?"

"Right." And he got out.

Turning over the engine, I saw the chief of police staring at me through a window. He watched as my boyfriend hustled down the street and I backed out of the parking place.

The high school was one of those modern miracles with plenty of brick and no windows. I parked in front, got rid of my gum—this was a school, you know—and went into the office and introduced myself, saying Roy Scruggs sent me to see Martha Perkins. The woman behind the counter nodded, then stepped over to a row of switches and flipped one, speaking over an intercom.

Martha Perkins came through loud and clear, saying any visitor would have to wait until she was finished with her classes. If the visitor cared to wait, she still might have students hanging around after class, but to send me back once the senior bell had rung.

The woman behind the desk smiled. "Mrs. Perkins is very set in her ways."

It was two-thirty and I really didn't want to cool my heels. The principal's office did not bring back fond memories. "Is there somewhere I can get some lunch?"

The woman gave me more than adequate directions to a local greasy spoon, as if she'd been embarrassed by being associated with Martha Perkins.

At the greasy spoon the waitress was shown a picture of Babe that I'd dug out of Donna's stuff. She said she'd never heard of anyone named Constance Delphine Parnell or "Babe" Parnell, but she'd just moved here to get away from the mess in Charlotte. The cook said a bunch of Parnells lived over in Indian Trail. There were a lot of turns and some mailboxes I'd have to watch for. The waitress wrote it all down.

I returned to the high school just as the senior bell rang and found Perkins' homeroom on the second floor.

Martha Perkins was an elderly, gray-haired woman, spry, alert. No hunched shoulders. She wore a red dress with small, yellow flowers. Her arms looked muscular and they were tanned, as was her face. A pair of glasses hung around her neck on a black cord.

Perkins had put those windowless walls to good use. Three of the four walls were covered with posters illustrating how people lived during colonial times. The other wall held a blackboard. While she discussed the Gettysburg Address with a student, I walked around admiring the artwork. If I ever had kids, they were going to get an education if I had to pound it into them.

"Yes?" asked Perkins from across the room.

I turned around to find us alone. I began weaving my way through the rows of desks. Contrasting to the drawings of colonial times was a TV on a metal stand by Perkins' desk.

The TV's program was fed by computer, listing daily and weekly asignments, spelling lists, and suggestions for extra credit, all on a continuous loop.

She snapped off both computer and TV. "Saves wear and tear on the arm, and the school board's chalk budget."

Perkins stood behind a desk old enough to be the one she'd begun her career with. It was scratched and worn, and spots in the wood had turned black from constant use. A stack of papers sat at one corner of the desk, and at the other, a thin book for recording grades. A cup from WBT radio held pens and pencils.

Gesturing toward the walls, I said, "Nice work."

"It makes the children think about how people lived during those times. But you didn't come to see me about my students' work, did you, young lady? You're not old enough to be a mother; just out of high school yourself, aren't you?"

I glanced at my blouse and slacks. "And I was hoping this outfit made me look grown up."

"Grown up for what, young lady?"

"To be taken seriously."

"I take all young people seriously until they prove otherwise." She gestured at the door. "But not Ronnie Oliver. He was doing a bit of apple polishing just now. If he spent half the time studying . . . Miss . . . ?"

"Chase. Susan Chase. I'm from Myrtle Beach." When she made no comment about the Grand Strand, I said, "Roy Scruggs sent me to see you."

"Roy Scruggs," Perkins said with a snort. "One of the worst students a teacher could ever have, and I've had some doozies. He could've been a teacher, Roy was that smart. But he drifted along, playing football and chasing every tart in Union County before the army drafted him. But he's made a decent enough police chief, so all's not lost."

"He seems to think a lot of you."

"Folks think anyone who can put up with today's kids qualifies for sainthood. I'll tell you this, Miss Chase, I didn't make it thirty years by being a saint. You have to stand up to young people, especially nowadays." She gestured at the desk in front of her own. "Now have a seat and tell me what can I do for you."

I told her I was trying to locate the dark-haired girl in the photograph. I laid the picture on the desk in front of her, then took my seat. In the picture was Donna holding Megan, and Babe Parnell. I couldn't find one of me with either Megan or Donna.

Perkins put on her glasses and sat down. She studied the photograph, then looked over the glasses. "I'm supposed to know this girl, is that what Roy said?"

"He said you knew just about every kid in Union County and might be able to help me find her."

The glasses dropped from the woman's face and she put down the photograph. "Now why on earth would he say something like that?"

"I have no idea, Mrs. Perkins."

"Miss. I never married."

"Yes, ma'am," I said with a nod. "Miss."

"Why are you looking for her?"

I hesitated. Roy Scruggs hadn't been anyone to muck around with. I'd learned that the hard way. Might be better if I played this straight. Sorta.

"I'm a private detective working in conjunction with the South Carolina State Law Enforcement Division, or 'SLED.' We're looking for a woman who calls herself Constance Delphine Parnell, a.k.a. Babe Parnell. She was last seen in Myrtle Beach a week ago." I gestured at the photograph between us. "That's supposed to be a photograph of her, ten years after you taught her."

"And the charge?"

Crossing my legs and sitting back, I asked, "Miss Perkins, do you know who this woman is?"

"I might, if you tell me the truth, and remember, I've sat across from more than one young person who's tried to pull the wool over my eyes."

"Er—yes. The truth."

"Is that so hard, Miss Chase?"

"Well, Mrs.—I mean, Miss Perkins, you might not believe the truth. No one else does, and I think it has something to do with my age."

"You tell me the truth and you won't have any trouble from me. But if you lie to me . . . ."

So I told her the truth, and by the time I finished, I was in tears. Not to worry. Perkins had a box of Kleenex and handed one to me. I figured it wasn't the first time this had happened to someone sitting in front of her desk.

"The rest room is down the hall on the right. After you've composed yourself, come back and I'll tell you what I know about Connie."

"Connie?" I sniffed, wiping the tears away.

"Yes." Perkins tapped the photograph. "Connie Parnell. That's the name of the short-haired girl in the photograph. The other girl I don't know. I assume she's the mother of your godchild. I taught Connie in eleventh grade. She was one of my better students and I was very proud of her, no matter what others might say."

6

When I returned to Perkins' room, a china cup of hot tea was waiting for me. Another cup sat in front of Perkins. I slid into the desk and picked up mine.

"Thanks."

"Think nothing of it. I usually have tea in the afternoon. Sort of a pick-me-up after a long day with the children." The old woman gestured at the paperwork stacked on the corner of her desk. "I don't take my work home. I know a single woman like myself isn't supposed to have anything better to do, but I have a farm to work." Flexing one of those tanned arms, she added, "The farm was left to me by my father. I was the only one who wanted it, and I couldn't find a husband who would work it. Actually, at that time of my life, the time a young woman usually gets married, well, at least when they used to marry in those days, that time fell after the world war, the second one, that is. Most of the men were either killed, maimed, or pretty well picked over, so I've tended my farm alone. But one day I won't show up for work and they'll send Roy Scruggs out to my place to learn what's happened. He'll find me lying across the pig trough or keeled over under one of the milk cows, or, hopefully, dead in my bed."

Perkins glanced at the door as a gaggle of gigglers walked by. "Those girls don't know how fortunate they are. Their parents will be able to afford college. Nothing like the first place I taught. That school was a farm-based income or your parents worked at the mill. About six years ago this side of the county began to change. I suppose you saw all the subdivisions sprouting up?"

I nodded that I had, then sipped from the cup. The tea was very good and didn't taste like any blend I was used to.

"The school board came to me and several others who'd spent their lives educating the young people of Union County and asked if we'd move to the new high school. Well, I for one was ready for a change." She took a sip of tea before continuing. "I'd become a bit jaded about knowing everyone in that part of the county, and with these new children there'd be less baggage. Or so I thought. The children in those new subdivisions have too much time on their hands, which gives them plenty of opportunity to get into mischief."

"Connie Parnell was one of these people?" Good tea aside, I really didn't want the history of Union County.

"No, Miss Chase."

There were no windows to gaze out of, so the old woman took a moment to stare through the door. You could hear kids up and down the hall. Occasionally, a locker door slammed off in the distance.

"Connie was one of my star pupils. She took a real interest in history. If I ever needed help after school, anything having to do with history, Connie was the first to volunteer. She even talked the yearbook advisor into allowing her to write a column of historical interest for the student newspaper. Sometimes the column was a bit preachy, as if the other students were supposed to take the same interest in whatever struck Connie's fancy, but that was later on."

"Something changed?"

"A second baby died."

"A second . . . baby . . . died?"

The old woman nodded. "Connie was a devoted baby-sitter and when she was only twelve the child she was sitting for died from SIDS. You know what that is?"

"Crib death. Babies die in their sleep and doctors have no idea why. Some think it has something to do with second-hand smoke. Others believe the child was probably born incomplete, but that's not something parents want to hear so SIDS stays shrouded in mystery."

Her head tilted to one side. "You're quite well informed for someone your age. Where did you say you went to school?"

"On the street. You say there was a second death?"

She picked up a pencil and tapped it a few times before going on. "What you have to understand is that when the first child died, Connie was so distraught that her family doctor recommended counseling so she'd understand it hadn't been her fault. The counseling continued for at least a year. I have to point out, the worst you could say that was wrong with Connie's family was that the girl didn't have enough time to be a child. There was an older stepbrother from a former marriage by her father, but Connie was responsible for the younger children when her parents weren't home."

"What about the older brother?"

"Living with his girlfriend. They later married when the girl became pregnant. After the death of the Wilkins baby, the first child who died from SIDS, Connie wouldn't sit, even for neighbors who understood the cause of death and offered their sympathy."

Perkins stared into the hallway again. The school was quiet now. It was after four. I was going to be late meeting Chad. Then again, he was probably searching for a thingamajig or a whatchamacallit for his mom. Perkins looked at me again and I was surprised to see she had teared up.

"Then Connie's older brother's wife asked Connie to baby-sit for their daughter who was only six weeks old."

"This was the woman who'd been living with the brother,

became pregnant, and then later married?"

Perkins nodded. "Laura. She had to beg Connie to sit that night. Laura and the brother had to be at a meeting with their counselor. They were having marital problems. I don't remember the brother's name. I never taught him. Anyway, Laura said Connie had been around the new baby all its life, played with it, so what could possibly go wrong?"

By now I was on the edge of my seat, stomach jammed against the writing platform, my tea all but forgotten. "What happened?"

"They came home and found Connie asleep on the sofa, and while the brother was waking Connie to take her home, Laura went into the baby's room and found the baby dead."

"Connie killed it?"

A severe look crossed Perkins' face. "Of course not, Miss Chase. Life is much more tragic than it is dramatic."

"Who examined the baby? There had to be an autopsy."

"There was, after the sister-in-law accused Connie of murdering her child. That was when the column in the school paper changed, as I told you."

"I don't care about the school paper." I could hear my voice rising. "I want to know the autopsy results."

But this was a woman who had spent her life around children and believed she could control her environment. She went on as if never hearing me.

"The column took on a sordid aspect, devoting itself to what people had done in their personal lives instead of their accomplishments: such as Thomas Jefferson's dalliance with Sally Hemings; Franklin Roosevelt's relationship with Lucy Mercer; and even that foolishness about Abraham Lincoln and Jefferson Davis being half-brothers because they were fathered within a few miles of each other."

The old woman sipped from her cup before addressing my concern. "All the coroner found were two crib deaths, and his findings were backed by the forensic people in Charlotte. But Laura wouldn't let it die . . . . That wasn't the proper choice of words, was it? Anyway, Laura never forgave Connie for her child's death. Their marriage went downhill and they finally divorced. Since then Laura has remarried—twice, the brother never again."

"When everyone was telling them to have another child and put the death of the first one behind them."

"Yes, Miss Chase. I'm glad you understand."

"I might understand what you've told me, but that doesn't mean I sympathize."

Now it was the old lady's turn to lean forward. "But don't you see, Connie needs your understanding, not your hostility. She's gone through a bad spot and it wasn't her fault. She doesn't deserve to be persecuted."

"Unless she's stolen someone's baby."

The woman sat back in her chair and stared at me.

"When was the last you heard from Connie?" I asked.

"When she was in college."

"Parnell went to college? You said her family didn't have any money."

"Scholarships, Miss Chase. Connie qualified because of her grades and her financial situation. I wrote a letter of recommendation myself."

"Where'd she go?"

"Rutledge College, just down the road."

"What year?"

She told me, and it turned out to be only four years ago. "And this was the last time you saw her?"

"Connie came by while she was attending Rutledge, but I haven't seen her since she graduated. I can understand why she might want to put Union County behind her. People's tongues do wag and people like you are one of the reasons they'll never stop."

"I have to find my godchild."

"A baby who no longer has any parents."

"She has grandparents."

"And from what you've told me, one grandparent has

Alzheimer's and the other is busy caring for her. Miss Chase, why are you doing this? It would seem your being an orphan would make you more sympathetic to Connie's plight."

"I wouldn't steal someone's godchild."

"'Someone's godchild.' Would you listen to yourself?" She paused to sip from her cup again. "And you have no proof. Why, you sat right there and told me the South Carolina State Law Enforcement Division only wants Connie for questioning. There are no charges pending, none any law enforcement agency would bring, unless a troublemaker raised them. If I were Connie, I wouldn't answer any of your questions. I wouldn't have anything to do with you. Connie Parnell has had to answer questions about babies all her life."

I tried another tack. "Did Connie have any friends while she was in school?"

She had to think about that. "Sissy Johnson lives in Florida now. She married a boy who became an Air Force mechanic. Haley Faulkner's still around. She's . . . let me think. She's married . . . no, she divorced Robert Hanna, then married James Penny. She would be Haley Penny now. Haley works in one of the stores downtown. I don't know which one. Robert would know. That's Robert Hanna, her ex. He has a service station on Main Street where the tour buses gas up because they can turn around in the parking lot next door.

"You're a good listener, Miss Chase. Usually I admire that in a young person, but in this case it means you'll probably succeed in locating Connie. When you do, please tell her I was asking about her, and if there's anything I can do for her, tell her she still has friends in Union County."

The chief of police was waiting for me when I left the building. He sat in a white patrol car under a gray overcast sky and rolled down his window as I crossed the parking lot. His breath showed in the air, as did mine. The arm of his brown uniform contrasted sharply with the white of his patrol car.

"A moment of your time, Miss Chase."

I stopped six feet from the car. A teacher came out of the school with a bulging briefcase, hurried down the steps, and then opened her car with a remote. I pulled my coat tight around me. The wind was picking up and the sun going down.

"Aren't you a little out of your jurisdiction, Chief? I'm in the parking lot."

"That's the new elementary school. I thought you might speak with me."

"But I don't have to, do I?"

"If you don't, I might have to take you in for questioning."

"And what would be the charge?"

"I'm sure I could think of something." He scanned the dreary sky. "I might have to arrest you for stupidity if you don't get in the car pretty quick. It's awfully cold out there."

I looked around the parking lot, felt the wind sear my face, and then walked around to the other side of the car. Three or four students sat on the steps, hunched over from the cold, waiting for rides.

I closed the door behind me. "My boyfriend's expecting me, and it's past the time we set to meet."

"I told him you might be a little late."

I leaned back. "You did?"

"That young man really cares about you. I don't think he wants to see you in trouble with the law again."

"I didn't know I was."

"Miss Chase, you make it hard for a person to reason with you and that's why I'm here—to reason with you." He shifted his heavy frame around so he could face me. This caused me to grab the door handle. The chief saw this. "Don't you ever let your guard down?" he asked.

"When I have, it's always ended up biting me on the ass."

"Then all I can say is that you're going to have an awfully lonely life."

"I was hoping to liven it up by telling folks about dangers to their community, the ones authorities don't police."

"Meaning Connie Parnell?"

"You knew about her when you sent me to see Martha Perkins. What's up with that?"

"I thought Martha Perkins, who's an old friend of Connie's, might make you see the girl has enough problems without you bothering her."

My hand slid off the door handle. "I'm not bothering anyone. I'm only looking for my godchild."

"Who disappeared when her mother's car went off the road and ended up in a creek during one of the worst storms to hit the Grand Strand since Hurricane Hugo."

"You do your homework, don't you?"

"Just as you do yours. Somehow you learned that Connie Parnell lived here."

"And I think she wants to be found and be punished."

He frowned. "Pardon?"

"Connie knew what kind of work I did. That's why she told me about being from Waxhaw and the controversy regarding Andrew Jackson's birthplace. So I'd remember."

He stared at me as if I was nuts. I'd seen the look before.

"You know I have every right to ask you to leave Waxhaw, considering your reputation and what you've been through lately."

"But not Union County?"

"No, but I would pass along my concerns to the county sheriff."

"Damn, but you people stick together, don't you?"

"Miss Chase, not only did I drop by to see if you had talked with Martha Perkins, but to tell you about a young woman from Stallings, a Miss Beth Horner."

"Mind if I smoke?" I asked, reaching for my purse.

"I certainly do." He glanced at the windshield, which was beginning to fog up. "I don't want to have to roll down the windows. It's damn cold out there."

"Then make it quick."

"Beth's mother could've gone to college, the woman was that smart, but she didn't and Mrs. Horner believed, rightly or wrongly, that marrying early in life ruined her life. She harped on this to Beth that if the girl didn't get a good education it would ruin her life, too."

This hit a little too close to home. I was beginning to feel the effects of my lack of education. Friends said it became worse the older you got.

"By the time Beth was old enough to go off to college she'd fallen in love. As you can imagine her mother was against the marriage."

"Saying it would ruin her life. That she should go to college." I was trying to hurry him along.

"The marriage never came about. The boy was a house painter and one day he hooked his ladder over a live wire—it was a metal ladder—and he was killed instantly."

"I'm sorry to hear that, but what does that have to do with Connie Parnell?"

"I'm getting there, just give me a moment. The next boy Beth became engaged to, well, driving home one night, he fell asleep at the wheel and ran into one of those quaint-looking mailboxes you see along county roads. This particular mailbox had a miniature plow mounted on it, and when the boy ran into the post, the plow flew off the mailbox, smashed through the windshield, and hit him right in the forehead. That young man's in a wheelchair, Miss Chase, and he doesn't remember Beth Horner."

"So Beth took her mother's advice and went to college."

He nodded. "Beth's happily married, has a job as a reporter at the *Observer*, and her first child is on the way."

"To whom she will preach the value of a good education."

"Yes, but you and I know Beth Horner didn't have to go to college to be happily married. She could've married the next young man who came along. The two accidents were totally unrelated and did not mean there would be a third."

"You think it's the same with Connie Parnell."

"Miss Chase, if there was something fishy about the deaths of those babies, Connie Parnell would be in prison now. I know for a fact her mother preached at Connie that she was responsible for her siblings while her parents weren't at home."

"Connie helped raise her brothers and sisters without incident—why couldn't she make the connection with her baby-sitting job?"

"She wasn't responsible for the sister and brother until they were in grammar school." He gestured at the school behind us. "I thought by visiting with Martha Perkins you'd learn whatever you needed to settle this in your mind."

"To do that, Chief, I'd have to locate Connie Parnell and see if she had Megan Destefani with her."

"And that's why I'm here. Do you still have the map they drew for you at the restaurant where you ate lunch?"

"Er—yes." This guy was definitely no yokel.

"Then follow the directions to Indian Springs and you'll find Connie's mother."

As I got out of the car, I forced myself to say, "Thank you, Chief. I appreciate your cooperation."

"You're welcome. Now I want you to drive into Waxhaw, pick up your boyfriend, and take that map and locate Connie's mother and ask your questions—on the QT. Then when you're through, I'd appreciate your leaving Union County and never coming back. And when you find Connie, perhaps you'll use those talents as a private detective that Lieutenant Warden says you have to shadow Connie a day or two and see if your godchild is actually with her. Then, when you learn the child is not with her, I hope you'll return to Myrtle Beach and let Connie get on with her life."

7

The Parnell home was a ranch-style house made of brick. It stood along a two-lane blacktop on a county highway near Indian Springs. There was a deep yard in front with no sidewalk. A gravel driveway led up one side of the property where several vehicles were parked. A porch ran along most of the front of the house, two straggly plants hung in pots, and in front of the porch, a row of stunted azaleas looked like they'd been at it for quite a while but with little success, or fertilizer. There wasn't a tree or bush on the property and the trim on the house could've used a coat of paint. The row of houses looked as if a small-time farmer had sold out and given a developer a corridor in which to plant this very small subdivision.

While Chad stayed in the jeep and listened to a news story he had found on talk radio, I pulled my coat tight around me, crossed the yard, and stepped up on the porch to ring the bell. I hesitated. A note was taped over the button asking visitors not to ring the bell because someone inside was sleeping. Yet when I tapped on the storm door, it opened so quickly I thought the woman must've seen me pull up.

She was a middle-aged version of Babe Parnell with the

same brown hair cut close to her head. Mrs. Parnell had narrow lips, dark eyes, and a nose that came to a point. But this was the older edition, with a puffy and lined face, slacks bulging at the hips, little or no waistline.

"Yes?" she asked, stepping outside and closing the storm door as noiselessly as possible.

"Mrs. Parnell, I'm Susan Chase," I said with a practiced smile. "I went to school with your daughter at Rutledge College. I was in the neighborhood and thought I might stop by and see her."

"You went to school with Connie?" The woman looked at the jeep parked in the gravel driveway.

"That's my boyfriend," I said, glancing in Chad's direction. "We're from South Carolina."

The woman's hand came up to her throat, then stayed there holding her blouse tight against her chest. "Gosh, I've never met one of Connie's friends from college. How did you find us?"

"I asked Martha Perkins. Chad and I don't have to be in Charlotte until tonight and I thought Connie and I might catch up on old times, maybe even go out to dinner." I flashed an even bigger smile. "Your family might want to come along."

"Martha . . . Perkins told you how to find us?"

"You know Miz Perkins, don't you, teaches at the new high school?"

"She was one of Connie's teachers. Truth is she taught me, Miss . . . ?"

"Chase. Susan Chase. I'm from Myrtle Beach."

A hint of a smile appeared on the woman's face. Good. I thought my face might break in half from all the effort.

"Well, I'm sure it's warmer down there than it is up here. Connie's not here, Miss Chase. I'm sorry you missed her, but I'll tell her you came by."

"That's a shame. I was looking forward to seeing her again." Gesturing at the jeep, I smiled. "Though I don't know how much fun it'd be for my boyfriend to listen to us gals gab about our college days. By the way, did Connie ever get that job writing for magazines?"

"Why, yes, she did." Parnell glanced at the door. "Miss Chase, I really can't ask you inside. My . . . friend's asleep in there. The kids aren't allowed to play the radio or watch the TV when Garnell's sleeping. He works the third."

"Oh." It was chilly as hell out here, but I needed more from this woman. I hoped she could stand it. "Connie didn't tell me you and your husband divorced."

"Separated really. You know how it is these days, you try and try, but things don't always work out." She glanced at the metal furniture on the front porch. "Why don't you and I set a spell. I'll get my coat. Be just a minute."

Before I could object, she disappeared inside, easing the door shut and leaving me to anticipate the joys of chatting on a porch where the wind chill factor dropped the temperature below freezing. I hoped *I* could stand it.

Chad stuck his head out of the jeep. "What's going on?"

I stepped off the porch to say, "Mrs. Parnell and I are going to talk." If her friend Garnell could intimidate kids into not playing the radio or watching TV, then he wasn't anyone I wanted to bother. "She's getting her coat."

"Aren't you cold out there?"

I shook my head, lying like a rug.

"When I see you're ready to leave, I'll crank the engine and have the heater going."

His concern warmed me considerably, and it wasn't until Mrs. Parnell and I were deep into conversation that my teeth began to chatter.

When Parnell returned, she was careful to close the door again. "I don't get to meet too many of Connie's college friends. Connie's probably embarrassed to come home, especially now that her daddy and I've separated."

Oh. I thought it might've had something to do with two dead children. We walked down the porch to the metal furniture. "Where is Connie these days? Do you have her address? Maybe I could write her."

Mrs. Parnell sat down and I took the seat next to her. My coat tried to snag on one of the rough edges, but I'd been prepared for that, holding it tight around me, more likely trying to keep from freezing to death.

"Connie travels a lot. I get letters and cards from all over."

My heart sank, but I kept my voice cheery. "You mean she travels out of the country. Connie has a job traveling around the world?"

"No, no, it's all here in the United States. Sometimes she gets to go to New York or California, but most of the mail is from this part of the country."

"You mean the Carolinas?"

"Mostly the South. Connie says people want to know the dirt on the South, so she has to talk to the locals to find her stories. Why, one year she spent the whole summer in that play on the coast, *The Lost Colony.* Another summer she reenacted the battle of Chickamauga in Georgia."

"That's how I remember her. When she was working on a project, sometimes she'd forget to eat."

"That's why we don't see her much. Connie loves history, Miss Chase."

"'Susan,' please. Does she ever call?"

"Sometimes. But you know how young people are, off in their own world."

"Did she get home for the holidays?"

Parnell nodded enthusiastically. "She did and seemed to be real happy. I was glad to see her that way."

"New boyfriend?" I asked with another smile.

"No. Nothing like that. She was headed for the beach. Now isn't that funny, the two of you that close and not knowing it."

"Did she give you an address where I can reach her there?"

"This was before she settled in. I haven't seen her since then, but like I said, I was happy to see things finally working out for her."

You mean Megan Destefani was working out for her. I didn't know how to tell this woman that her baby stole babies. How do you tell any mother that? "Then you have no idea where to reach her? You don't have any of Connie's letters with her return addresses?" I had to be bold here or this conversation was going nowhere fast.

"Connie never put an address on her letters, because she really had no home base. She moves from one town to another, staying only long enough to write her articles, then moving on."

"Gosh," I said, sitting up and trying to shake some feeling into my limbs, "that doesn't sound like any way to live, moving around all the time." I gestured at the jeep. "I wouldn't want to lose my boyfriend." I smiled, giving her some of me, hoping she'd share some of her daughter. "You know how it is with men, you have to baby them."

"I know what you mean. We have to tiptoe around while Garnell's sleeping. I could give Connie your address when I hear from her."

"I'm sure she's still got it. I haven't gone anywhere. I certainly don't lead an exciting life like Connie." Before she could ask what I did for a living, I asked, "So with all this moving around I guess Connie never married?"

"No, she didn't, but she did have a baby."

"She did?" A hollowness opened in my chest.

"Yes, but I don't think the father would marry her because Connie never brought him home to meet us."

"When was this?" And where had that child been while Babe Parnell had been living along the Grand Strand?

"A couple of years ago."

"Then Connie has a . . . two-year-old." Why hadn't Roy Scruggs or Martha Perkins mentioned this? Was everyone in on this scam?

"No. The baby died."

My throat constricted. Icy fingers reached for my heart.

After glancing at the house again, Parnell said, "The baby's death broke up Connie something fierce. She had to come home to live with us. But the only thing that was good for her, and I could see this myself, was for my little girl to get back on the road and working again. I encouraged her to leave."

Or Garnell did. I glanced at the house myself. I couldn't see Babe Parnell taking any crap off a live-in boyfriend. "When was this?" I asked.

"Oh, a year or so ago."

I shuddered. I was going to be sick right in front of this woman who'd given birth to such a monster. Babe Parnell had stalked Donna Destefani and stolen her baby to replace the one she'd lost. "I'm . . . I'm sorry to hear that. You say the baby's father wouldn't marry Connie?"

"Probably because she moved around all the time. I didn't ask, but I think the father was someone Connie became friends with when she did articles about the Natchez Trace. Connie was up and down the Trace a whole summer."

"Got to be . . . got to be a tough way to raise a kid."

"Yes, yes, I know, but these days girls do just about whatever they want. Have a baby without the father." She shook her head. "I couldn't. People would talk. People still talk about . . . ."

When she didn't continue, I asked, "Sounds like you didn't know she was pregnant."

"I think Connie was embarrassed to tell us. After she had the baby she came to see us. The child was almost six months old."

"Gee, that's a long time to wait to bring home a grand-child."

"And I just hated it, not being able to see my grandbaby. But I understand. Union County isn't a place where Connie has fond memories."

"You're talking about the crib deaths?"

The women sat up. "Connie told you about that?"

I nodded.

"It weren't her fault, but people talk like it was. That's why she doesn't want to live in Union County. The coroner said there was nothing funny about those two babies' deaths, even when Laura, that's Connie's former sister-in-law, was running around telling everyone that Connie had killed her baby."

"It's must've been tough on Laura, too." I really didn't know where to go with this, but I wanted to keep the woman talking while I collected my thoughts. Megan was in much more danger than I'd ever imagined.

Parnell was talking. ". . . know Laura's baby was dead, but nothing could bring her back, so I didn't appreciate her going around bad-mouthing my child. Mark didn't appreciate it either. Mark's my son. He divorced her, but Laura won't let go and still talks about how all her marriages have soured because of my little girl killing her daughter."

"And then . . . another baby died."

Parnell nodded. "She'd showed that baby all around and then the baby ups and dies."

"Died? What—what did the baby die from?" I was almost afraid to ask.

"Why that crib death so many children seem to die from these days. I just hope Connie can find a man who wants to marry her."

"But that wouldn't suit Connie, would it? She stays on the go."

Parnell glanced at the house once again. "There has to be give and take in a marriage, and that's what my husband didn't understand. He can't work two or three jobs and not pay the family any attention. After a while it doesn't matter that the bills are getting paid, other things around the house aren't being attended to. That's part of a husband's responsibility, too."

And as if on cue the man handling that chore appeared at the other end of the porch. He let go of the storm door and it closed with a thump. If Garnell wanted to get some sleep, maybe he should adjust that door.

"What's all this yammering?" The live-in boyfriend was a rangy guy, wearing a pair of jeans and long hair but nothing else. Both arms had terrific definition and sported tattoos lacking any color. A sure sign the jerk had picked up those tattoos in prison. The fact he was crossing a concrete porch barefoot didn't seem to bother him. "Can't a man sleep around here?" There was a couple of days beard on his face and his skin had a swarthy color to it.

Mrs. Parnell leaped to her feet, blocking the access to me between the railing and the metal furniture. "I'm sorry if we woke you. We were talking out here so we wouldn't."

"Well, you done it. Women running their mouths. Don't you have anything better to do? Are you gonna fix my dinner? And I don't want the same ol' slop you've been fixing lately."

"Do you have a fan?" I asked from behind Mrs. Parnell. I was on my feet and unbuttoning the front of my long coat.

He glanced over the woman's shoulder at me. "A fan? What the hell would I need a fan for in this weather?"

"Run a fan in the room where you're sleeping and it'll drown out the noise. That way the kids can watch TV when they come home from school."

Garnell looked at his girlfriend. "Just who the hell is this kid, Shirley?"

"She's a friend of Connie's. They went to school together."

"Well, I don't want her around here. I don't like her mouth. I think she's sassing me."

"No, sir," I said, fed up with the passivity of this woman. "If I were sassing you, you'd know for sure."

"Why you snotty-nose little brat. You're doing it again." He jerked Parnell out of the way.

As he came for me, I placed both hands on the railing and vaulted into the front yard where I landed beyond the stunted azaleas.

Chad came out of the jeep in a hurry, leaving the door

open. "What's going on here?"

Garnell glanced at my boyfriend as he headed down the porch and for the steps. "I'm running your girlfriend off my property, fella. What's it look like?"

"It looks like you're picking on a girl." Chad moved to intercept Garnell before he reached me. "Maybe you'd like to try me first?"

"Chad, this isn't the time or place . . . ." I'd gotten all I was going to get out of Shirley Parnell. Chad, however, was in his protective mode, and why not? He'd spent the afternoon shopping while I'd done all the heavy lifting.

As Garnell came down the steps, Chad brought up his fists. "I don't want any trouble here, Mister, but if that's what it takes, I'm ready."

Shit. I doubt if Chad had been in two fights his entire life and probably both in grammar school. And though the two men were of similar size and build, Garnell looked street tough.

"Leave him alone, Garnell. We're leaving."

"Not until I teach your boyfriend here some manners. Come to a man's house when he's trying to sleep and raise a racket—"

"This isn't your house. It still belongs to Shirley's husband."

"Garnell," said Shirley Parnell from the porch. "Let them be. They didn't mean any harm."

"Hell, no," he threw over his shoulder. "Not before I teach this little bitch and her boyfriend some manners."

"Rednecks don't have manners, so what could you possibly teach us?"

"Susan, let me handle this."

When Garnell glanced at Chad, I pivoted around on one foot and threw the other at Garnell's knee and came down hard. There was a cracking sound and Garnell shrieked, grabbed his leg, and hit the ground. Rolling away, he tried to bounce back to his feet, which only reinforced the image we were up against an experienced brawler. His leg, however, wouldn't support him and he went down again. He looked up to see if Chad would take advantage of his predicament. Shirley Parnell stood on the porch, staring at her man on the ground. Their relationship would never be the same, and probably for the worst—for her.

Garnell tried to get to his feet, but his knee didn't work. "You bitch! Look what you done to me. I think you broke something."

"You want us to help you into the house?" asked my boyfriend.

"I don't want any help from you."

Chad looked at the woman on the porch. "Ma'am, he could freeze out here. Could you get something?"

"I don't want any fucking help from you people."

"You'd rather sit here and freeze?" asked Chad.

Garnell set his jaw. "I'll do it."

"Mister, we've got to get you into the house. The sun's going down."

"You come any closer, boy, and I'll pull you down here and kick your ass."

"Stay away from him, Chad."

"And you stay out of this, Suze. You probably started this with your mouth."

"She did, taunting me in front of my woman."

"And I kicked your ass, too." I didn't feel the cold. My blood was boiling. I'd had enough of Union County.

"Susan, go sit in the jeep while I help this man into the house."

Garnell's teeth had started chattering. "Listen, bud—bud—buddy, I don't need your help."

"I'll get you a blanket," said Shirley, heading inside.

Garnell wrapped his arms around himself. It didn't help. He continued to shiver. As I walked over to the jeep, I saw Chad hold out a hand. I didn't want to look but couldn't help myself.

Garnell unwrapped an arm and waved him away. "Get—get away from me!"

"Chad . . . ." I pleaded.

"Susan, I told you to get in the jeep."

I did. If my boyfriend wanted to get his butt kicked, that was his problem.

On the road in front of the house, a car slowed down and its passengers wiped fog off their windows not to miss the scene playing itself out in the Parnell's front yard. Hopefully, Chief Roy Scruggs wouldn't hear about this. Chad and I still had to pass through Waxhaw on our way out of town.

Looking up from turning on the heater, I saw that Chad had Garnell under one arm and was helping him into the house. Shirley had come to the door with a blanket. She threw it over his shoulders. The woman was followed to the door by two teenagers: a boy and girl, and the girl was smiling. Garnell cursed and waved them away as Chad helped the injured man into the house.

A few minutes later, Chad reappeared at the door, saying something to Shirley who had followed him out of the house. The teenage girl stood behind the storm door and evaluated my boyfriend, and from the look on her face I could see she liked what she saw. I was about to climb down from the jeep and adjust another attitude when Chad shook Shirley's hand, said good-bye, and then spoke to the smitten teen before leaving the porch. My boyfriend approached the jeep from the driver's side so I scooted over to make room for him.

Climbing in, he said, "Now if you'll keep your mouth shut, I doubt we'll have anymore problems."

"Sometimes it's not my mouth that sets people off."

"No. Kicking them in the shin will do it every time."

"The side of the knee, Chad. I wanted to incapacitate him, not piss him off."

"I think you did both."

Chad drove down an empty Main Street, past all the

antique and consignment shops, to Hanna's Exxon Service Center. Just as I'd been told by Martha Perkins, there was a gravel parking area beside the station where tour buses could park. A triple A sign hung in front of the station, along with all the other major credit cards. Parked beside the two-bay building was a huge wrecker, one large enough to tow a tour bus. Two stocky guys, one in jeans and a jacket, the other in coveralls, were moving small wire stands of merchandise into the bays. Robert Hanna turned out to be the one in the coveralls. When Chad pulled in, I climbed down and told him to keep the engine running.

Hanna saw me coming. "Ma'am, I hope it's something quick 'cause we're closing."

I flashed him a smile that would melt Popsicles. "You know Martha Perkins?"

"Her pickup giving her trouble again?"

"She sent me to see you. Said you'd know where to find your ex-wife, Haley."

"Yeah," he said with a frown. "I know where she is." The other attendant had stopped moving racks of oil and additives into the service bay. To him, Hanna said, "Go on, Bob. Finish up so we can get out of here."

"I'd appreciate it if you'd tell me where to find her."

"Do you mind me asking why, Miss . . . ?"

"Chase. Susan Chase. I'm doing some research about the people in that high school class, trying to locate as many of them as we can."

"I was in that class. Did Miz Perkins mention that to you?"

"Sorry," I said, with another smile, "but it's about the girls, not the boys."

Hanna snorted. "It's always about the girls these days, ain't it? All the programs on the TV, everywhere you look, it's always about women. That's why Haley and I aren't married any longer."

Standing there freezing my butt off, I wasn't really all that interested in his opinion of modern culture, but the subject had given him a head of steam. "Haley thinks I'm old-fashioned because I didn't think she should be going out all hours of the night with her girlfriends."

"If you didn't, maybe she shouldn't," was about the best I could come up with to keep him talking.

"I was always at home, if I wasn't here." He gestured at the bays where Bob was lowering the doors. A set of rattling chains made Hanna raise his voice. "After putting in a day here—you have to be here early for the tourists—I was ready to go home, have a bite, and watch some TV. That's how come I know what's on the tube, and it's nothing but what women would watch, hardly ever a ball game, but that didn't interest Haley. All she wanted to do was barhop, sometimes in Charlotte, mostly at the Boar's Head. 'B-O-R-E-S Head' is what I call the place. Bunch of people trying to impress each other how they're getting ahead of each other in Union County. And that's where you'll find my ex, out there drinking with James Penny, her new husband."

That's all I needed, but Robert Hanna wasn't through. "None of those people has two dimes to rub together." He inclined his head toward the station. "I'll have this place paid off by the time I'm forty. And what did Haley think of that?" He spit to the side, startling me. "She said I should loosen up and have a good time. I reckon she found her good time with James Penny. He tried out for the Panthers and didn't make it, but while he was with them he sure did learn how to party."

"I certainly appreciate your help. Where do I find the Boar's Head Lounge?"

He gave me directions. "Need any gas?" he asked as I took my leave. "You ain't gonna find any gas out there and I'm about to shut down my pumps."

Matter of fact we did, and I learned why Robert Hanna would have his station paid off by the time he was forty. Not only did he fill the tank, but he and Bob cleaned the windshield, checked the tire pressure, and found one needing some air. Chad insisted on paying for the gas, and while we were at the station, Hanna pressed one of his business cards in my hand.

"You have a cell phone, Miss?"

I nodded.

He glanced at my jeep, an old red thing closer to pink these days. "I don't want to tell you your business, but I'd watch traveling on these back roads this time of night. You break down and you're going to have an awful cold walk home."

The Boar's Head Lounge was a free-standing building at one end of the strip mall which included a Food Lion, a pharmacy, and an El Cheapo service station.

"I thought Hanna said there wasn't any gas out here."

Inside the kiosk, a glum-looking woman huddled in front of a small black-and-white TV.

"To him I guess there's not."

Chad and I fit right in with the after-hours crowd in the restaurant, which had a special on prime rib—don't they all? On the wall behind the bar hung a huge boar's head, and under it, a mirror and a row of liquor bottles. We took seats near an ornate window with gold-tinted glass. Most people sat in front of a fireplace where a huge fire blazed away.

"How are you going to do this?" asked Chad, noticing the customers sat in fours and fives.

A couple of waitresses handled the tables where men wore business suits, women wore dresses. A bleached blonde appeared to be having more fun than the others, and she sat in the lap of a huge guy with a thick neck and arms that strained the fabric of his pullover.

After a waitress took our order, I asked, "Is the blonde on the big guy's knee Haley Hanna?"

The waitress wore a short skirt, a tight blouse, and a bright smile. "You're behind the times. Haley and Robert were divorced a year ago. She's married to James Penny. The football player."

"The guy who tried out for the Panthers?"

The waitress nodded. "That's him."

"Then," said my boyfriend, cutting in, "buy the happy couple another round and put it on our tab."

"I'll surely do that," said the waitress. "Want me to tell them who you are?"

Chad shook his head. "Just point us out."

The waitress nodded and left for the bar.

Chad realized I was staring at him. "You're not going to have all the fun, Suze."

"Then, if you really want to make this work, look deeply into my eyes and ignore the Pennys so one of them will come over and find out who we are."

"You sure that'll work or are you just trying to seduce me?"

"Take it any way you want, big fella."

Glancing at the table where the Pennys sat, Chad said, "Speaking of big fellows, I don't think you're going to handle that one with a kick in the shin."

"To the knee, Chad. A shin kick would've only pissed Garnell off. The kick to the knee put him out of action."

"And you're proud of that?"

"I don't know what you mean."

"That one of these days you might bite off more than you can chew. You know, there's not a woman alive who can take a man if he wanted to beat the hell out of her. It's upper body strength you girls lack."

"Uh-huh. You wait until I pin you to the bed tonight."

"You're going to use your upper body strength?"

"That and my other upper body strengths."

The conversation went along in that vein until the waitress returned with our beers. On her tray were a couple of drinks for the Pennys. When she took them over, the blonde looked in our direction, but it was more of an effort for her husband. He had to shift his own bulk around and bring his wife with him.

Chad and I toasted them with our beers, then returned our attention to each other. Minutes later, the blonde fumbled her way over to our table.

"Do I know you?"

"I don't think so, Haley."

She pulled over a chair and sat down. Chad took his seat again. He'd stood with the arrival of the Penny woman. Chad's always doing that when I leave a table or arrive. I've tried to break him of the habit, but I haven't tried very hard.

"Why'd you buy us a drink? Is this some new approach for network marketing?"

"I went to school with Connie Parnell at Rutledge. My boyfriend and I were looking at antiques, and while we filled up at the Exxon, I asked where I could find Connie. Your ex said if anyone would know, it would be you."

Though she was tighter than bark on a tree, she managed to push away from the table and stand up. "You're no friend of Connie's."

"How do you know that?" asked Chad.

She turned on him, and the sudden motion almost made her lose her balance. "Because Connie didn't have any friends at Rutledge. She said the girls hated her because of what happened to that baby."

"You mean the babies who died in Waxhaw?" I asked as casually as possible.

"No—the dean's baby that drowned while Connie was baby-sitting it."

8

At breakfast the following morning, Chad brought me up-to-date on the little boy stuck in the well. Chad said the story had been on the TVs in the antique shops. It was all people could talk about.

The trapped boy was in Ft. Smith, Arkansas, a place on the Oklahoma/Arkansas border. Three kids had been playing near an abandoned factory and one had fallen into a pipe system and gotten stuck about twenty-five to thirty feet down. The rescuers wanted to lower food to him, but the pipe took a funny turn, making that impossible. Someone had proposed monkeys to perform the feat. That's all I could take and went to bed. Chad had stayed up with the TV turned down low. My boyfriend's the type who thinks if he keeps tabs on the world, somehow it won't spin out of control.

I lost my appetite as he described one failed attempt after another to send food down to the trapped boy. The kid was only thirty feet away but hungry and crying for his mother. Backhoes had been brought in and operators were waiting for plans of the pipe system, due to arrive this morning. After I watched Chad wolf down, not only his breakfast but mine—I guess that's why you watch the news. It helps the digestion—we stopped by the local paper and learned which dean's child had drowned, then drove to the school.

Rutledge College is a small coed school of fewer than five thousand students. Rutledge remained a women's college until the early 1970s, and the Boomers I know who went there, before the college turned coed, think the years spent at Rutledge were the best years of their lives. Without men on campus, only women could run for office, be elected, and solve the problems of an all-female student body.

I left Chad in the jeep and found the dean's office in a brick structure with enough ivy to obscure entire walls. The building was at the end of a grassy commons lined with more buildings built with still more red brick. The entrance to the building was through huge wooden doors, which made you figure the female student body had had pretty good upper body strength before the turn of the century. In each of these oversized doors, two regular-sized glass ones had been cut. They were much easier to open. The dean's office was on the third floor, and Louise Moultrie was in conference when I arrived.

"Do you have an appointment?" Moultrie's secretary was a thin woman with cinnamon hair. "The dean doesn't see anyone without an appointment."

"I think she'll see me."

"And your name is?"

"Susan Chase."

"And your business with the dean?"

"That would come under the heading of confidential."

The woman sniffed. "Then you'll have to make an appointment, and our students receive first priority." She gestured at kids sitting around the room. They were dressed quite well, for students.

I bit my lip. The longer I waited, the farther Megan slipped away. Taking an envelope from my purse, I handed it to the woman. "Would you see that the dean receives this at the end of her current appointment."

The woman held the envelope as if it might be from the Unabomber. "I'll see what I can do."

"Look, I think it would be smart of you—"

"Threats will get you nowhere, young lady." The secretary fingered the envelope. "I might open this myself, for security reasons."

She didn't get the chance. The door to the dean's office opened and a student came out, followed by Louise Moultrie.

Moultrie was a short woman with hair much longer than should be worn by a woman her age. She smiled at the young woman who was leaving her office and told the girl to focus more on academic work than on extracurricular activities. Moultrie wore a skirt and blouse bulging with her size, and over that, an expensive sweater. The skirt was gray, the blouse white, and the sweater royal blue; a real Marina Rinaldi customer. Moultrie smiled at me as the secretary called a name and a young woman wearing a long-sleeved blouse and floor-length skirt collected her books, got to her feet, and crossed the room.

"Dean Moultrie," I tried.

"I'll be right with you. Where are your books? You're not to waste time while waiting to see me."

"But that's not why—"

"Dean Moultrie," said the secretary, "she brought this by." The thin woman handed the envelope to the dean. "She says it's confidential."

Moultrie took the envelope. "Very well. It'll be a moment, Miss . . . ?"

I had to clear my throat to speak. "Susan Chase. I'm from Myrtle Beach."

"Well, give me a moment with Lou Ann and we'll see what we can do."

As the dean followed the young woman into the office, she slid a nail under the flap of the envelope and closed the door. From our side of the door we heard a thud, followed by a scream from the young woman in the floor-length skirt. And how do I know it was the girl in the long skirt? She appeared at the door, using the jamb to stay on her feet.

"Dean Moultrie . . . Dean Moultrie . . . ."

The secretary leaped from her chair and rushed around her desk. I followed her. Behind us students cautiously stepped to the doorway, and seeing the dean prostrate on the floor, rushed out of the waiting room.

The secretary was bent over her. She had the dean's hand in hers, patting it. "Dean Moultrie, Dean Moultrie?"

The girl in the long skirt didn't know what to do. Her hands fluttered around. "We hadn't even started talking. She . . . gave this little gasp and fell to the floor. I mean, I didn't actually see her fall. I heard the gasp and didn't think anything of it . . . ." She glanced at her pack, which sat in one of the chairs in front of Moultrie's desk. "I guess I was thinking about what I was going to say."

I pulled a small tube from my purse and joined the secretary on the floor. Breaking it open, I tried to stick the tube under Moultrie's nose.

The secretary grabbed my hand. "What are you doing?"

"It's only smelling salts."

"But—but she might be having a seizure."

"Have you ever known the dean to have a seizure?"

When the thin woman shook her head, I stuck the smelling salts under the unconscious woman's nose. Moultrie's head jerked away, then she waved at the smell, trying to push it away. She opened her eyes and looked from one of us to the other.

"What—what happened, Priscilla?"

The secretary said she didn't know.

"You fainted," I said.

Her eyes focused on me. "Who'd you say you were?"

"Susan Chase. I'm an investigator from Myrtle Beach."

Moultrie looked around as if trying to understand what she was doing on the floor. While Priscilla tried to explain, I picked up the photograph, slid it back in the envelope, and returned the envelope to my purse.

"I—I don't know what happened," stammered the secretary. "You closed the door and the next thing I knew Lou Ann was screaming."

Lou Ann repeated what she had said before the dean had been revived. The girl's hands appeared to be washing themselves without the benefit of water.

I said to the secretary, "Why don't you clear the dean's calendar for the rest of the morning? We have some catching up to do."

Moultrie grasped our arms so we could hoist her bulk into a sitting position. "I was looking at that . . . photograph, then . . . ." She focused on me. "You know something about Connie Parnell, don't you?"

"Yes, ma'am, I do."

"Then, Priscilla, do as she says. Clear my calendar. Miss Chase and I have business to attend to."

"But the president's luncheon is at eleven-thirty."

"If I can make it, I will." The heavy woman wanted to be helped to her feet.

"You stay right where you are," I said. "You've had quite a shock."

"Yes, yes, you're right." Gracious as any sorority girl, she asked, "Would you like something to drink?"

"Coffee—black—would be fine."

"Priscilla, would you mind?"

The secretary regarded me warily as she stood. "Of course. Anything for you, Dean?"

"No, thank you." Moultrie saw the girl in the long skirt at the door. "Lou Ann, I will see you tomorrow. Make another appointment before you leave."

The girl nodded quickly and turned to go.

"And Lou Ann . . . ?"

"Yes, Dean?"

"Inform the other students that putting so many students

on probation finally took its toll. That should focus their attention on their studies instead of gossiping about me."

"Yes, Dean. I will." She turned to go.

"Don't forget your backpack, my dear."

The girl nodded and hurried by us to claim her pack from the chair before disappearing through the door.

"I want to stand," said Moultrie.

"As long as you warn me if you feel woozy."

"That I'll do."

I helped her stand, then walked the woman over to the desk. Her seat was a high-backed chair that, when swiveled around, overlooked the grassy commons. I took a seat in a straight-backed leather chair on the other side of an orderly desk. On one side of the room were rows and rows of books. On the other, shelves displaying African artifacts: masks, spears, shields, and the like. The curtains behind Moultrie were thick and complemented the wine-colored wall-to-wall carpet.

"I come from money, Miss Chase."

"Believe me, Dean, it shows."

Moultrie fumbled around in a drawer and dug out a bottle of Jack Daniel's, along with a glass. While she poured a shot, she said, "You should've seen this place when I moved in. The most ordinary of offices, but with a spectacular view. I asked permission to make these changes, even had the shelves made to order, but I had to do it bit by bit so the others wouldn't be jealous. The shelves were installed during Christmas break. I really don't think anyone's noticed. The draperies and carpet were installed during summer vacation."

The dean downed the contents of the glass, then looked at the wall to her left. "The African pieces date from a time when I was much younger, more idealistic, and quite a bit thinner."

Moultrie's secretary returned with my coffee and placed the cup on the corner of the desk, interrupting my gaze at the bottle of Jack Daniel's.

"Hold my calls, even if it's the president. Tell her an emergency has come up."

The secretary glanced at me. "If you need me, I'll be right outside the door."

"Don't worry about us. We have something in common, don't we, Susan? May I call you Susan?" When I nodded again, she added, "And you are to call me Louise."

Priscilla wasn't so sure and took her time leaving.

After the door closed, Moultrie said, "Priscilla is very loyal, and for good reason. I make it possible for her family to spend a week at my condo at Hilton Head each summer." After another shot from the bottle, the Jack Daniel's was returned to the drawer. "Okay, I'm ready. You've come to see me because another baby's died."

"Almost, but how'd you know?"

"Nowadays I make it my business to know. There were two deaths in Waxhaw. I didn't know about them when I employed Connie Parnell as my baby-sitter."

"How'd it happen: your daughter's death, that is?"

Moultrie leaned back in her chair, taking the glass from the desk. "Connie was an excellent student who came from a poor background and qualified for scholarship money. By the time Connie was a sophomore, she was baby-sitting for everyone. She never went home, and she took jobs none of the other students would take: real brats. There are some awfully confused parents on our faculty, Susan. People raising their children in a manner that will not help them in the Real World. Later, and here I mean, after Katherine's death—Katherine was my daughter—many in our community breathed a sigh of relief. What had happened to Katherine could've happened to their child." Moultrie shook her head. "People really trusted that girl. That's why she's so dangerous."

The dean stared at her desk. When she looked up I could see her eyes were damp. "For the longest I couldn't get my mind around the fact she was a murderess. When Connie didn't return to school, I hired a private detective to check on her and he learned about the cover-ups in Waxhaw."

"Cover-ups?"

"You don't really think Connie is as pure as those people in her hometown make her out to be?"

"Absolutely not."

"It ruined my marriage. Tad was a commercial banker and commuted into Charlotte. We thought we had the perfect life at Rutledge."

She glanced at a door built into one of the walls. I hadn't noticed the door, but I was aware of the fact that she hadn't told me how her daughter had died.

"I lost Tad because I wanted to get to the bottom of this." She leaned forward, placing the glass on her desk. "What has she done now?"

I told her everything I knew about Babe Parnell. I forgot about my coffee. Time passed, and suddenly someone was knocking on the door. Chad opened the door and stepped inside, followed by Moultrie's secretary.

"This young man says he knows the Chase girl."

"This is my boyfriend, Dean Moultrie. He's helping me investigate this case because the authorities don't take it seriously. His name is Chad Rivers."

"Good to meet you." Moultrie pointed at the empty chair besides mine. "Have a seat. You may leave, Priscilla. Everything is under control."

The secretary saw things differently. Moultrie's face was a mess. While I'd related my story, especially about losing Megan in the swamp, the dean had disappeared in her private washroom. In there I heard her throw up. She was headed for the rest room again.

"What about the president's luncheon?" asked Priscilla.

Moultrie stopped, one hand on the knob of the private room. "I've already told you the rest of the morning belongs to Miss Chase." She glanced at Chad. "And her friend." She disappeared into the rest room.

"What's going on?" asked the secretary.

"Don't worry," I said with a cheery smile. "The dean and I are just catching up on old times."

"But she fainted—"

"Some of those times were rather rough."

The secretary nodded, as if understanding, then glanced at the rest room, where we heard water running. With another glance at us, she left, closing the door behind her.

Chad sat down. "What's going on, Suze? You've been here forever."

"You remember the newspaper accounts that said Moultrie's daughter was being baby-sat by Parnell when the canoe they were in overturned and the baby drowned. Moultrie believes it was intentional and that Parnell planned it all along."

"Sweet Jesus, but that woman is sick." He stood when the dean reentered the room. "Why's she doing this?"

"Because she's nuts," said Moultrie, answering my boyfriend's question. She pulled the bottle of Jack Daniel's from the drawer, poured another drink, and downed it in one gulp.

Gee, Susan, maybe this is how people feel when they watch you drink.

After returning the bottle to its drawer, Moultrie popped a mint into her mouth and came around the desk. "Come on, you two. There's someone I want you to meet." As we walked toward the door, Moultrie gripped my arm. "You know, my dear, your godchild is dead. You must be strong."

"I don't know about that. Two years ago Parnell showed up at home with a baby and told her mother it was hers. According to Shirley Parnell that baby lived until it was two. I'm hoping the same thing's happened to Megan and that Connie hasn't grown tired of having her around."

9

On our way to another of those imposing, ivy-covered red brick buildings, Louise Moultrie filled us in on the woman Chad and I were about to meet.

"Olivia Deitz took her training at Johns Hopkins. On full scholarship," she added, the temperature showing on her breath. "When Ollie graduated she practiced privately in Charlotte for several years until I convinced her to join our staff. Now, each day from one until four, she answers questions on the radio."

The dean saw our quizzical looks as we crossed the commons. "She's quite good. The radio station built a broadcasting booth in her home where she fields calls every afternoon." Moultrie beat Chad to the door of the building and hauled it open. "She's quite a celebrity on campus. When kids have problems, they go to Ollie. Some of them even call her show."

Then it was up the stairs to the fourth floor, passing students who appeared to think Moultrie was a celebrity herself. They nodded and greeted her by name. Then it was down a hall and past several classrooms and a bulletin board filled with job offers from across the country.

At the rear of a narrow office sat a slender black woman who had good cheekbones and was impeccably dressed in a white blouse, navy blue blazer, and skirt. She shared her office with a secretary and a tweedily-dressed fellow. Papers, books, and bound reports were everywhere, stacked on shelves, in chairs, even on the floor. Every surface was covered until you reached the very rear of the room, where the slender black woman's desk was immaculate. A Day Runner lay at the upper right-hand corner, a pen nearby—not a ballpoint but a fountain pen. Behind her and through the window lay the grassy commons.

Louise Moultrie wove her way through the desks and clutter. There was no greeting from the tweedily-dressed fellow, only a curt nod; then he was on his feet and out the door. The black woman looked up as the three of us marched down the narrow aisle. She was reading a thick book, and when she laid it down, I could see it had awfully small print. To tell you the truth, being in close quarters with this much education was slightly intimidating.

"Ollie, we need a moment of your time." Moultrie took a seat in the chair beside the desk and motioned for Chad and me to do the same.

Deitz glanced at her watch. "I have class in ten minutes, Louise."

"You may skip it after hearing what Ms. Chase has to say."

The black woman was staring at me, but I didn't know that until I had slid a stack of papers out of a chair and carefully placed them on the desk of the tweedy fellow. I rolled the chair over and sat down.

"Ollie," Moultrie said, in a tone sounding as if it was meant to end a long-running argument, "this is Susan Chase."

Deitz looked at me, then Chad, who was carrying a chair from the front of the narrow room. The secretary's chair, as the young woman was no longer at her post.

"Susan's a lifeguard at Myrtle Beach," explained Moultrie.

Deitz nodded. She was plainly puzzled. Why not? The woman had a lot of catching up to do.

Moultrie leaned forward, touching the therapist's knee. "Susan has some grand news." The dean sat up. "Well, not grand in the normal sense. It's more tragic, but still . . . . Susan, why don't you tell Ollie what happened at the beach. Oh, and this is her friend, Chad Rivers."

The therapist nodded to my boyfriend.

Having told this story more than once, I soon fell into its rhythm, giving only the bare bones about Megan's disappearance. That wasn't good enough for Moultrie. She interrupted several times to elaborate on various points, especially when it came to Connie Parnell.

At the end of my tale, she said, "You see what this means, Ollie."

Instead the therapist spoke to me. "What you say about the disappearance of your godchild, this is true?"

"It is."

"Then you are probably as puzzled at my role in this affair as I was when you and Mr. Rivers came through the door."

Moultrie sat up. "Oh, gosh, Ollie. I'm sorry. I should've explained—"

"Why don't you let me?" asked her friend.

The dean gave a quick nod, then slid back into her chair. I glanced at Chad and saw him staring at Moultrie. I could tell he didn't like what he saw.

"Louise came to me as a friend—we were both involved in the same professional association—to discuss this matter."

"And it's worked out marvelously," said Moultrie, beaming from her chair.

"I've been trying to help Louise, on an informal basis, work her way through her daughter's death—"

"Murder! And what Susan tells us proves that Parnell killed Katherine."

Everyone in the room stared at Moultrie, then Deitz went

on. "According to what Ms. Chase has said, there is that possibility."

"You're damn right." Moultrie brushed down a fold in her skirt. "And for the life of me, I don't know why you ever doubted me. It was murder plain and simple and now we've got the proof to nail that woman."

I could only stare at the dean. That happens when I run into someone who's even more gung-ho than myself.

"Ms. Chase," asked Deitz, "you say the South Carolina Law Enforcement Division—SLED, as you call it—has an all-points bulletin out for Connie Parnell?"

"Under the name of Babe Parnell. Her father gave her that nickname."

"Did you confirm that her father gave her that nickname while in Waxhaw?"

"Uh—no." It had been damn cold on the Parnells' front porch and Garnell had been such an asshole.

"But she is wanted for questioning?"

I was nodding when Moultrie said, "It'll be more than questioning now that we have four murders to question her about."

"There's no proof that Megan Destefani is dead," said Chad from behind us.

We all looked at him.

"We assume she's dead . . . ."

Moultrie gave him a withering look.

"Well," said Chad, "we don't."

"That's right," said Deitz, weighing in on my boyfriend's side. "We need to stick to the facts. Louise, I've warned you about that in the past."

The heavyset woman shifted in her seat like she had ants in her skirt. "This is ridiculous. For over a year you've told me to cool it. This is not the time to cool it. Susan, what's the name of that SLED detective who's helping you with this investigation?"

"Lieutenant J.D. Warden."

"He's simply doing his job," clarified Chad.

Moultrie ignored him. "Ollie, if you're going to pooh-pooh my concerns, I think it's time I found someone else to confide in."

"Louise, that is always your choice. You are not even a client, only a friend. All I've said is you must proceed carefully. Remember what happened the last time you rushed to judgment?"

"My judgment wasn't wrong and this proves it."

"Still, you have to admit, it was a disaster."

Moultrie stared at the floor as Deitz explained.

"When Louise questioned the accident report—"

The dean's head snapped up. "Accident, my foot."

"Very well, Louise. Perhaps it would be best if you told Ms. Chase and Mr. Rivers what happened the last time you asked too many questions about Connie Parnell."

"No, no, you tell them. I'll—I'll try to control myself." Her breathing became fast and furious. At any moment she might hyperventilate. Now I understood why the secretary and the professor had made a hasty departure.

Deitz glanced at her watch. "I would like to continue our discussion, but I have an eleven o'clock class."

"And you have to be at the president's luncheon," said Chad when he stood. "Maybe we should get together another time."

"When?" Moultrie looked at us one and all.

"I have my program from one until four. Perhaps I could talk with Ms. Chase then."

"Very well, and I'll be there."

Moultrie, Chad, and I parted ways on the wide stoop of the administration building, where students came and went. "You'll be here, won't you, Susan?" asked the dean.

"Of course," I said, watching my breath form on the air on this dank and dismal day. It was overcast and the wind whistled through the commons.

As we shook hands, Moultrie's secretary came through

the glass door fitted into one of the humongous wooden doors. She took the dean's hand and led Moultrie into the building. All around us young people, hunched over in jackets and coats, hurried for a door, any door, just to get out of the weather. Although the temperature was a little more than forty degrees, we were suffering in the chilly dampness.

Once the door closed behind Moultrie, Chad said, "That woman has a screw loose."

"Her daughter drowned."

"And she won't let it go."

"I'm having trouble myself."

"So I've noticed." He looked across the commons where students hustled toward their classes. "It appears we have some time on our hands. How do you want to spend it?"

"Why don't we talk with the police? They might know something."

"And they might give us a different perspective than Louise Moultrie's?"

"If they'll talk with me."

"Why wouldn't they?" he asked with a grin. "You're working with SLED, aren't you?"

"I'll certainly make them think so."

A young woman approached us. A yellow cashmere sweater had been thrown over her shoulders to protect her from the cold. It wasn't doing the job. The woman openly shivered. "Miss Chase?"

"Yes?"

"Doctor Deitz would like to see you."

"I thought she had an eleven o'clock class."

"She wants to talk with you before she goes on the air this afternoon."

"In her office?" Now I remembered. This woman was the department secretary who'd hastily exited the communal quarters when Moultrie had appeared.

The secretary handed me a piece of paper from a yellow-lined pad. "Take the street behind this building and you won't have any trouble finding her house. It's a bungalow."

The local cops' story differed little from what we had learned from the dean, except that Katherine Moultrie's death had been filed as an accident. For that reason both Chad and I were looking forward to what Olivia Deitz might have to say.

Deitz's place had a low roof and wide porch with no furniture. It was built of large river stones held together by concrete. Shrubbery grew around the bungalow and a gravel driveway led to the rear. Chad pulled into the driveway and parked. As we climbed down from the jeep, I saw a gray BMW parked in the rear, a satellite dish mounted on the chimney, and smoke coming from the chimney. On either side of the door was a large picture window with drawn curtains.

Deitz answered the door on the first ring. She had changed into slacks and a cardigan sweater but still wore the white blouse. Inside we found overstuffed furniture, walls decorated with African artwork, and a large woven rug covering a hardwood floor. A decent fire crackled in the fireplace. It felt good after the weather outside.

Deitz gestured to the sofa facing the fire. "Have a seat, Ms. Chase, Mr. Rivers."

"Susan."

"Very well," Deitz said with a nod. "Would either of you like coffee?"

We both said we would. The fire looked wonderful. Chad opened his coat so the heat could hit him. Deitz saw this as she headed to the rear of the house.

"You can toss your coats on one of the chairs, Mister Rivers."

"Chad," said my boyfriend.

"Chad," Deitz threw over her shoulder. Changing her clothes and her surroundings hadn't changed the woman's attitude. We weren't welcomed, only tolerated.

Chad helped me off with my coat. "Are people always this weird when you conduct your investigations?"

"Only the ones who have something to hide."

"What in the world would this woman have to hide?"

"That's what I intend to find out."

Deitz returned with a coffee pot and three mugs. She put them on the coffee table in front of the sofa, then took a seat in an overstuffed chair. The fire crackled invitingly.

Deitz noticed my boyfriend staring at her. "Is there something on your mind . . . Chad?"

"Er—no . . . ." He glanced in my direction.

"He's curious as to what you haven't told us about Louise Moultrie."

"Sugar or milk?" she asked.

I shook my head and took a mug.

"Good." The shrink poured her own. "If the coffee's good, there's no reason for sugar or cream. Don't you find that to be true?"

"I've never found coffee that good," said Chad, opening the sugar bowl and dumping a spoonful into his mug. As Deitz and I watched, he mixed the crystals into the black liquid without tasting the coffee.

"This is very good," I said, after sipping from mine.

"Thank you."

Chad said something rather lame about how good the coffee was. His comment was ignored by Deitz, who leaned back in her chair and held the mug between her hands. She looked into the fire.

I said, "We noticed how she was being handled. Why would people do that?"

Deitz looked at me. "Why would a radio station place a satellite dish on top of my house and allow me to continue my program from here instead of Charlotte?"

"Moultrie's that good?"

"Yes, and believe me, if I weren't qualified, I'd be history.

My professors warned me about entering this specialty. There are few black psychotherapists because white people will not listen to what we have to say. I mean, how could I relate? When I told my colleagues I was returning home to the South, they said I'd better look for a teaching position. They were right. My practice never exactly thrived."

She sipped her coffee. "One evening at a professional meeting it was announced that a radio station was looking for a new psychotherapist to replace the one moving away. I know what you're thinking: You're wondering why, if I had all these difficulties with my career, would I think I could be the psychotherapist for thousands of listeners who were mostly white?

"Then one of those things happened that so often our lives turn on. We call it luck because, as human beings, we cannot bear that life is such a series of random happenings. I received a call from the radio station. The program director had read my resumé and wanted me to interview for the job. I almost made the mistake of telling him I was a person of color when he went on to say the initial interview would be conducted by phone. It was a radio talk show, after all. I must admit, after having the color of my skin held against me in the past, I enjoyed the process. Anyway, the program director had people call and ask advice over the phone."

"Who were these people?"

"Some were phony. But there were also your garden variety of worries, fixations, or frustrations. Later I learned that one of my callers was the wife of the program director and she felt I'd helped with a difficult teenager in the family. Anyway, what these people reported back to the program director would determine the finalists."

"So they didn't know you were black until you showed up on their doorstep, and because you were, they were afraid not to hire you."

"Yes."

"What you did was dishonest," Chad said.

The therapist leveled her gaze at him. "You should spend a few days as a black person, Mister Rivers."

I leaned forward, practically placing myself between the two of them. "I've been trying to make Chad understand why people don't take me seriously. It's not just my age."

Deitz nodded. "I had two strikes against me."

"Louise Moultrie helped you get this job?"

"And I'll be forever in her debt for nagging me to send in my resumé. But there's something else, and that's what I want to talk to you about." She put down her mug. "Louise was making progress—"

"Until I entered the picture."

"To put it bluntly—yes."

"Well," I said, putting down my cup, "that can't be helped. I have a godchild to locate."

"If Megan Destefani is actually missing."

"What do you mean 'if she's missing?'" asked Chad. "Babe Parnell, or Connie Parnell, stole her."

"But what if you are wrong?"

"What do you mean—wrong?"

I leaned back into the sofa. "Doctor Deitz believes the Moultrie's child's death was truly an accident."

"An accident?" Chad looked from one of us to the other. "What are you talking about? The dean's daughter was murdered and if we don't catch up with this 'Babe' or 'Connie' person, or whatever she calls herself, the same's going to happen to Megan."

"Neither baby in North Carolina was murdered," Deitz said, "according to the authorities."

"I don't understand . . . . Susan, what's going on here?"

"What Doctor Deitz is saying is that she doesn't think it was anything—"

"But a tragic accident," interjected Deitz.

"And you'd like us to move along so you can continue helping Moultrie get over the death of her child."

"I understand Louise passed out when you merely showed

her a photograph of Connie."

"Word travels fast around this place," Chad said.

I pulled the photograph from my purse and placed it on the coffee table.

"Yes," she said, glancing at the photo. "That would be Connie Parnell."

"Did you know her when she was a student?"

"The president asked me to counsel her. She didn't want anything on the record."

"What record?" asked Chad.

"People don't want therapy showing up at an inopportune time in their future. The president was concerned because Connie had her whole life ahead of her."

"What did Connie tell you?"

Deitz leaned into her chair, taking her mug with her. "Confidentiality is the basis of all successful psychotherapy, Ms. Chase."

"I really need your help, Doctor."

Deitz shook her head.

"Is that your final answer?"

She nodded.

"Deitz, this afternoon, while you're on your radio show, I'm going to meet with Louise Moultrie, and I wouldn't be surprised if she offered me money to make sure I stayed in touch with her."

"You would do so, even if it was detrimental to her mental health, your desire for revenge is that strong?"

"You've got that right, and I'm the delivery girl."

"Ms. Chase, Louise Moultrie is very important to this college. The grade point average at this institution has risen half a point since she became dean. That may not mean a great deal to you, but half a point on a scale of 4.0 is quite an achievement for any academic dean."

"Connie Parnell is a threat to children and I'm going to stop her."

"But you have no proof."

Touching my stomach, I said, "This is all the proof you need when you're raised on the street."

After glacing at my stomach, she said, "And based on that feeling you are willing to hunt down Connie and persecute her, and along the way, raise the hopes of Louise Moultrie."

"If Connie doesn't have Megan, she'll be rid of me once and for all. All I need is an opportunity to observe her."

The woman stared at me as I drank more of her delicious coffee. Enough time passed that I had a chance to read the titles on the shelf behind the woman. Weird. I'd actually read some of the books. Harry Poinsett would be proud.

She put down her cup. "Ms. Chase, my radio program begins in twenty minutes."

I stood up. "Don't let us keep you. I'm sure the president's luncheon is over by now."

As Chad stood, Deitz let out a sigh. "Sit back down. You, too, Mister Rivers." It was Deitz who now stood. "I have to make a sound check fifteen minutes to the hour. Give me a moment." She disappeared into the rear of the house.

After she was gone, Chad said, "Suze, this is so weird . . . ."

I leaned into him, letting him give me a good, long hug. "I don't know what I'd do without you, my man."

He pushed me back where he could see me. "Are you serious?"

"Of course." I gestured at the doorway where Deitz had disappeared. "You're reminding this woman of what normal people think."

We sat there, cuddling in front of the fire until we heard footsteps on the hardwood floor.

Once she was seated again, Deitz said, "Because the South Carolina State Law Enforcement Division is concerned—"

I waved her off. "Whatever."

Daggers shot from the woman's eyes, but she quickly regained her composure. "The fact is, Ms. Chase, Connie Parnell thinks she's cursed."

"Cursed?" asked Chad, sitting up.

"And that's why you inquired into her past, wasn't it?" I asked. "Otherwise you would've treated the Moultrie baby's death as an accident."

"Well, Connie has had some bad luck."

"I'll say," said Chad.

"Were there other incidents—involving Connie?"

"Absolutely not. Connie Parnell had an exemplary record at Rutledge."

"How did she say the accident happened?"

"Connie had baby-sat for the dean and her husband before. They're divorced now. Katherine's death did that, and for the same reason I'm worried about Louise."

"Taking out an eight-month-old baby alone and with no life vest, you approve of that?"

"Connie was an experienced canoeist. No one goes on the lake without being checked by security. And they all wear vests."

"But not a baby?"

"Ms. Chase, what you have to understand is that canoeing is something not only Connie and other students were fond of, but Louise and her former husband."

"The Moultries took their baby out in a canoe?" asked my boyfriend.

"Yes," Deitz said to him.

"Sounds damn irresponsible, if you ask me."

"Looking back, yes."

"Did anyone see the accident?"

The therapist shook her head.

"And you don't see anything suspicious about that?"

"I try to bend over backward to give a person the benefit of the doubt."

"But that could be considered—" started Chad.

I cut in. "How did Connie say it happened?"

"She had the baby in a baby carrier at the end of the canoe. Katherine started crying and Connie tried to crawl forward to reach her. There was a picnic basket between them. Crawling over the basket, Connie slipped and her shoulder hit the side of the canoe. The canoe tilted, flipping the baby and her carrier into the water. Connie went in after her, but the lake is quite deep at that point and the water's not very clear. She never found Katherine and finally crawled across the upside-down canoe and lay there, screaming for help. Other students tried to locate the baby, but all they came up with was her blanket. The rescue squad had to drag the lake to locate the body."

"It didn't float to the surface?" asked Chad.

"No, Mister Rivers, it did not." She looked at me. "As I try to explain to my patients, some loose ends in life are never tied up to our satisfaction."

"And Connie's condition," I asked, "after she was brought ashore?"

"Hysterical."

"Saying something like 'not again, not again'?"

The therapist's face hardened. "She said nothing of the sort. Nothing the police or the security people from the school mentioned."

"You talked to them."

"Of course. I take my responsibility to this institution very seriously."

"Then Connie's saying that she believed she was cursed only slipped out during your first—"

"Second session with her."

I leaned back on the sofa. "What do you think is wrong with her?"

"I think . . . I think she had an unfortunate childhood with the deaths of the two children. She has tried to over-compensate by baby-sitting more than the norm, taking on children no other sitter would spend fifteen minutes with. That puts her at risk. Connie's first therapist told her it was like riding a horse. You have to get back on when you fall off or you'll never ride again. The girl took that to excess."

"This is quite a change from when she was a teenager,"

suggested Chad, still staring at the woman.

"Connie is of childbearing age. She certainly didn't see herself in that light when she was a teenager."

"And while she tries to change her luck, more children die."

Deitz said nothing.

"Where do you think her head is at this time?" I asked. "Connie's, that is."

"If she did steal your godchild, she might be trying to make everything right. And that would mean your godchild is still alive."

"And if she killed the two children in Waxhaw and Katherine Moultrie here at Rutledge?"

"She still needs help—"

"Into an early grave," said my exasperated boyfriend.

"That, Mr. Rivers, would not be an appropriate solution to any problem."

"Does Connie know she's sick?" I asked.

"It's a compulsion Connie has, trying to rid herself of what she considers this so-called curse."

"And past actions are the best predictor of future actions?"

Deitz nodded. "Usually."

"Connie no longer has the child she showed up with at her house during the holidays."

The woman sat up. "I was not told about this."

"We learned that in Waxhaw. From Connie's mother."

"Then I would talk to the authorities if Connie had a child that did not belong to her . . . ." Deitz shivered and looked into the fire, probably wondering why these flames could not warm her. If I was right, this woman had allowed a cold-blooded killer to run a game on her.

She looked at me. "A person such as this—"

"Connie is all you need to say, Doctor," I said. "It's part of the healing process."

The woman's eyes became colder than any weather outside. "Connie would feel a compulsion to kidnap children over and over again to prove she could care for them."

"Then why kidnap them only to later kill them?" asked Chad.

"There are two compulsions at work here. One demands Connie get back up on that horse and ride again and the other tells her that she's worthless. Connie is quite torn."

"I'll say," commented my boyfriend. "That woman needs help."

"She certainly does," said Deitz, returning her attention to me. "But that's not what your girlfriend has in mind, is it, Ms. Chase?"

10

Since I live alone and don't report to anyone, I didn't call home when we finished at Rutledge College. But my boyfriend did, and his mother told him I was to call a Lieutenant Warden at the Grand Strand Law Enforcement Center. Mrs. Rivers probably had some other choice words for her son who associated with a gal who answered to the police. But if she said anything, Chad didn't let on. He simply held out the phone.

"You need to call Lieutenant Warden."

"What?"

I'd been lost in thought, staring out the window of the restaurant where we'd eaten lunch, wondering what to do next. The phone was near the register where Chad and I haggled over who'd pay the bill. We settled on dutch. Taunting me from a television were pictures of a backhoe working to free the boy trapped inside the pipe. But I was in South Carolina, having a decent meal while that boy was starving to death in Arkansas. And haggling with my boyfriend over who should pay the frigging bill.

"Warden left word with my mother," added Chad.

"He did what?"

"I don't suppose he thought you'd check in . . . ."

"But I might've checked my machine! You know, Chad, I can retrieve my messages from here."

His hands came up, including the one holding the phone. "Hey, don't slay me. I'm only the messenger." He looked to where people sat on stools at the counter, all watching TV. CNN was reporting from Ft. Smith, some middle-aged blonde by the name of Casey Blackburn. "Er—Suze, I think I'll have another cup of coffee."

Snatching the phone out of his hand, I said, "Yes. Why don't you!"

"Want to use my phone card?"

"I have my own, thank you very much. I bought it from Donna at CVS."

Chad nodded and beat a hasty retreat to the counter, where our waitress was pleasantly surprised to see my boy-friend return. She smiled broadly as Chad took a stool at the counter.

The moment I was connected with Warden, I exploded. "What the hell do you think you're doing, leaving word with Chad's mother for me to call you?"

"Just trying to reach you."

"Well, I don't appreciate it!" The old man behind the register glanced in my direction, then went back to ringing up someone's tab.

"I left several messages on your machine."

"Next time wait for me to call . . . you."

"Chase, can you stop long enough to listen to what I have to say?"

I stopped and listened, but all he said was, "So, what have you learned?"

I told him. "That's it? You just wanted to know what I found out? I could've told you when I returned."

"Then you still have no proof Constance Delphine Parnell has done anything illegal."

"No, but—"

"Chase, would you let me finish?"

After taking a breath, I said, "I'm listening."

"You have two crib deaths in North Carolina and the drowning of the Moultrie child at the college?"

"And Megan Destefani still missing."

"Uh-huh."

"Don't give me that 'Uh-huh.' There's still the child that Parnell brought home who later died. I don't know how she fits into all this. Connie's mother said she thought the child was fathered by a man her daughter met while writing articles along the Natchez Trace. Maybe you should check that. It happened less than a year ago."

"First I've heard about that. Where's the baby? Did her mother say?"

"The baby's dead by now, I would think."

"You think? What kind of investigation are you conducting up there?"

"I'm not . . . ." I had to stop because my breath was coming fast and furious. "I'm not doing this for you."

"Or very professionally either. Go on. What else?"

"What else—what? There's nothing else to report. Are you telling me to hang it up and come home?"

"No. I want to know if you're going to listen to what I have to say without butting in."

"I said I was listening."

"But you have also interrupted several times. I swear, Chase, if you'd only take direction—"

"From you, I suppose."

"From me, Harry Poinsett, your boyfriend, but you can't take anyone's advice, can you?"

"I'm up to here with advice," I said, making a motion over my head that Warden had no way of seeing. Again the old man at the register glanced at me.

"You know what, I agree with your boyfriend."

"About what?"

"I think it would be a good idea for the two of you to enter counseling, especially you, Chase."

I glanced down the counter and saw my boyfriend talking with the waitress. She was kind of cute, if you like them on the thin side, and Chad was probably telling the woman our innermost secrets. Lt. Warden cracking on me from Myrtle Beach—how else would he know about the counseling? And Megan . . . where was Megan? There was a pain in my chest and I couldn't feel the phone in my hand. What was happening to me?

I was on the floor with my head between my knees. The old man from behind the counter held me upright on one side, Chad on the other. When they allowed me to raise my head, I saw the concern on their faces. The waitress bent over, offering me a glass of water with one hand and a paper sack with the other.

"Susan," asked Chad, "are you all right?"

People crowded around me. No one was watching the TV.

"Give her some air," said the old man, letting go of my arm and standing up.

Chad remained beside me as the people backed off.

"What happened?" I asked.

"I was having a cup of coffee when I heard someone shout."

"That was me," said the man who'd been operating the cash register. "I thought you were talking with your folks with all the fuss you were making. All of a sudden you dropped the phone and slid to the floor. Kids and their parents—I've seen it happen before."

The phone was over my shoulder and someone was squawking through the earpiece.

"You stay right there, Suze." Chad took the phone and told Warden it was best that Warden speak with him. "Yes, yes, I'll tell her."

I barely heard him. I was using a brown paper bag to control my breathing.

Chad handed the phone to the old man, who hung it up.

"Bad news?" asked the old man.

"Not at all, but it does come somewhat as a shock."

"What did . . . what did he say?" I asked.

"Tell you when we get in the jeep. You just sit there and rest for a moment."

Most of the crowd was drifting away, returning to the reports from CNN.

"Is she going to need this water?" asked the waitress who still held the glass.

"I'll—I'll take the water." I gave up the paper sack and took the glass.

Chad helped so I could drink it, then smiled. His smile made me feel better than any glass of water.

"What did Warden have to say?"

"Not until we're in the jeep."

"Chad, I want to know!"

People turned and looked again.

Chad's face was grave when he said, "Lieutenant Warden found another kid who died. And Connie Parnell was involved."

In the jeep, with the heater on full blast, he asked, "What happened in there, Suze? You don't know anything Warden told me, yet you passed out."

"I just . . . . I just got pissed, that's all."

"At Warden."

"At Warden and a few more. What's this about another child dying?"

"But Lieutenant Warden was only trying to help."

"He was trying to give me advice."

"Which, of course, you wouldn't take. Really, I don't think—"

"You know, Chad, I really don't give a shit what you think. I want to know about this other dead kid."

"Susan, what's wrong with you?"

"What's wrong with me?" I could hear my voice becoming

shrill. What the hell did it matter? If I wanted to be shrill, I'd be fucking shrill. "I'll tell you what's wrong! Warden told me that we should go to counseling—after he called your mother—and I passed out in front of everybody in the fucking restaurant. Isn't that enough?" I realized my hands were shaking. I gripped the dashboard and leaned forward, gasping for breath again.

"Warden knows about the counseling?"

"Because you fucking told him . . . that's why."

"Susan, please. Watch your language."

"Fuck my language! You told him, didn't you? You told him we should go to counseling."

Chad reached for the stick shift. "I may have mentioned something about it."

I put my hand on top of his, holding us right where we were. "You're broadcasting our relationship to everyone. You tell your mother, Dads, and now Warden. Chad, you have to learn to keep a confidence."

His hand came off the stick and away from mine. "And why's that? So I can be a private detective? I don't want to be a private detective. I prefer building boats. It's simpler. You build the boat and if people want to buy it, they do."

"And who runs sales? Who convinces people they should buy your precious toys?"

"People need diversions from the stress of everyday life. What does it matter if it's a boat instead of a sports car? You look for runaways."

"Looking for runaways is my job."

"Well, it stinks as a job, if you want my opinion. The people you meet, the chances you take." He glanced at the restaurant. "If I hadn't been here, I don't know what would've happened. I don't even know what I'm doing here. You parked me in those antique shops, then the library when you went to see the dean. Every time I make an appearance you've either got some redneck trying to kick your butt or a woman's passed out from what you've just told her. What kind of work is that?"

"The truth upsets people."

"And the thought of counseling upsets you? Hello." When I didn't reply, Chad asked, "Did you ever think all this hostility's not normal?"

"This hostility's gotten me where I am today. I'm not on drugs, I've never been pregnant, and I've never sold my body to make ends meet. I think I've done pretty fuck . . . pretty damn good for someone who's raised herself."

"And you had a good deal of help along the way, admit it."

"What in the hell are you talking about?"

"That uncle you lived with in Florida until you were old enough to return to South Carolina and claim your father's boat. And Harry Poinsett who has spent hours educating you. Now J.D. Warden, who wants to instill in you a sense of normalcy instead of idiocy when you handle investigations."

"I know what's normal. I watch the afternoon talk shows."

"And that's probably where you learned to toss everything off with a joke."

"I wasn't joking."

He stared at me. "You're serious. You've learned things from TV. I never actually believed . . . ."

"Where would an orphan learn how to act? My mother walked out on us before I turned thirteen, and that uncle you said I lived with, he was in a full body cast when I arrived in Florida. Sure, he was glad to see me because I waited on him hand and foot. And Harry Poinsett was going through his divorce and didn't have time for me. And as for Warden, what about Warden? Did he get a hit on the computer?"

Chad had to stop and think, mentally changing gears. "When he began to get all these phone calls he went to the computer and ran her."

"Calls about Babe Parnell?"

"Calls about you."

"Me? What are you talking about?"

"I'm talking about the Waxhaw chief of police and Doctor Deitz. Deitz talked with J.D. before we arrived at her bungalow."

"And he told her?"

"As much as it might surprise you, Warden asked her to cooperate. Did you ever consider Warden might've made it work, that it wasn't all you?"

"Not in the time before she was going on the air."

"Suze, you can't run roughshod over people's feelings. This sharp edge of yours—it's something people can't handle."

"Can we move past this?" I wanted to know about this latest child who'd been killed. Time was running out for Megan, just like it was for that boy in the pipe in Arkansas.

"Susan, I can't do this alone. I need a referee. I need someone to call time out." He looked out the driver's side window. "Like when we get into one of these arguments."

Suddenly it was too close in here, in part from the heater, mostly from the conversation. I wanted to tell this guy he came from a family that represented a class of people I usually worked for, and that sometimes I had to return their money because I believed their children were better off away from their parents. I twisted the handle of the jeep and pushed back the door. Air rushed in. I shivered and not only from the cold.

"Close the door before you freeze."

"In a moment."

I wondered if I should have a cigarette and realized it was the first time I'd thought about having a smoke in a long time. What was up with that? But I didn't want to go there. Next I'd be agreeing with people who said I shouldn't be so foulmouthed.

"We've got to get going, Suze. To Spartanburg."

It was the specificity of the destination that reached me. "Where?" I asked, turning around.

"Spartanburg—where the other child died."

Spartanburg, South Carolina, is a town of a hundred thousand and is known for being the home of Roger Milliken, the textile baron. He, along with several other families, have controlled the growth of the area during the last fifty years. So if you don't like the growth pattern, take it up with Mr. Milliken. I only mention this because the woman we were looking for worked for Milliken and lived in a trailer park a few blocks from one of his mills. The trailer park lay two hundred feet down a lane, and at the end of the lane, the park sprawled in front of us—in darkness. Being a woman I have a thing about the dark. Some of the best and worst things have happened to me in the darkness.

It appeared the owner of the property had sold the rights to the land on the four-lane, then developed the property to the rear for all it was worth. Mobile homes were slammed in there. We had to skirt a couple of cars coming out, making even wider ruts in an already unruly dirt road.

The trailers were old and filled to capacity. Cars and pickups were parked along a circular road, there wasn't a tree or bush in sight, and where the street lights hadn't been knocked out, you could actually make out one home from the other.

"I never understood how people could live like this," muttered Chad.

"Careful, fella. If it wasn't for my father's shrimp boat I'd be living in a place like this."

"I'm just saying these people could go to school and better themselves."

"If you're a gal and have children, school is out of the question, except for your kids, if they don't get knocked up like ol' mom did."

"They could go to the library, do something. When you read about famous people who've lifted themselves up by their bootstraps, you learn that they spent a lot of time in the library."

"Times like that were much simpler, like when Edison could suggest that they simply remove the slip of paper that prevented the telegraph bell from ringing."

He glanced at me. "You have an answer for everything, don't you?"

"For what I've experienced—yes."

"And you're quite conscious that I come from that other world, aren't you?"

"Very much so, my dear."

"Think the twain shall ever meet?"

"If we work at it."

"Good." He leaned over and kissed me. "Because I love you, Susan Chase."

Hearing him say that made me tingle all over, and it didn't hurt that his tongue brushed my lips, causing that familiar hollow excitement in my stomach.

"You love me, too, don't you, Suze?"

"You know I do, baby. I didn't even crack wise about never having met Mark Twain."

He poked my shoulder. "You dog." He glanced at the park and its shadows. "How do we do this?"

"Since there's no sign saying where the resident manager lives, I knock on doors."

Chad surveyed the darkness. "I don't think I like that idea."

"People will open up to a gal more than they will to a guy, especially in this neighborhood."

"Then I'll be right here, shadowing you."

"I wouldn't have it any other way." I flashed a big smile, opened the door, and climbed down from the jeep.

Viola Kelly was the woman I was looking for. According to Lt. Warden, her daughter had been run down and killed in this trailer park, and Connie Parnell had been the baby-sitter. The way cars lined both sides of the dirt road, it could've happened anytime, not necessarily after dark.

Why had Parnell come here? Was she looking for more children to kill?

I climbed the steps of the nearest trailer and knocked on the door, wondering if they could even hear me. Their TV was really blaring. The door swung open and an old man stood there with a napkin hanging from his shirt collar.

No, he did not know anyone named Viola Kelly, and would I kindly go away and leave him alone so he could finish his supper and watch the news. Didn't I know there was a kid stuck in a well and a water line had been severed by a backhoe?

I shuddered and stepped back, almost off the small porch. I moved away from the edge. This was no time for mistakes, and certainly no time for broken ankles. Just find Megan.

At another trailer, a tight-lipped woman shook her head and closed her door in my face. At a third, no adults were at home, only a chunky teenager, wearing a robe pulled tightly around her as if she had hurried to the door. The girl didn't have a clue as to who I was looking for. She was stoned, and as I tried to make myself understood, a guy yelled from inside. "Mickey, close that door. I'm freezing." For that, the boy would have to be buck naked. I could feel the heat pouring out the door, tainted by the odor of kerosene.

Across the street, a minivan honked its horn. Moments later, a girl flung back the door of a trailer, leaped down from the door, and ran to the van. She carried a sports bag.

I left the stoned teenagers and hustled over to the minivan, where I knocked on the driver's door. The woman's back was to me, making sure the dark-haired kid got in. A blond girl sat in the front seat with her mom. Startled by my knock, the mother, also a blonde, jerked around and peered at me through the glass.

"I was wondering if you could help me."

Behind her, the side of the minivan door shut. Only then did the woman lower her window a couple of inches. She had a frantic look about her—I hadn't done that by tapping on her door—and it did nothing for the gaunt look many middle-aged women develop when they continue to diet and exercise. She was probably married to some guy losing his hair, both wondering what other tricks life had in store for them.

"I'm looking for Viola Kelly."

The blond woman shook her head. "I'm sorry. I wish I could help you, but I just come here to pick up a soccer player." She lowered her voice to add, "And believe me, if we didn't need her to fill out the roster, I wouldn't be here."

"I know Viola Kelly," hollered the dark-haired girl from the rear of the van. "I go to school with her daughter."

She left her sports bag and came forward to lean between the two front seats. The driver gritted her teeth. When she'd signed her kids up for soccer, no one had told her this kind of sacrifice would have to be made.

"Could you tell me where?" I asked.

The little girl was eager to please, and I wondered if her attitude and playing ability would be sufficient to lift the poor dear out of here. The blond girl in the front seat would have no trouble attending the college of her choice, but this eager girl was going to need some very long bootstraps.

"Better than that," the girl said. "I can show you."

From the minivan she directed our jeep around the trailer park. By now the black-haired girl had climbed into the front passenger seat. The driver's child made way by scooting over, and now the blond girl sat rigid, as if about to go over the first dip of a roller coaster.

The dark-haired girl pointed to a trailer where another van was parked. Next door a man wearing a heavy coat and sock hat worked under the hood of a pickup. A light connected to an orange cord ran out the door of his trailer.

"That's it," shouted the soccer player, leaning forward.

As soon as she pointed out the trailer, the mother stepped on the gas and they were out of there, flinging the black-haired girl back into her seat.

I got down from the jeep and walked past the other van. The neighbor working under the hood ignored me. I couldn't blame him. He wanted to finish and get back inside. The temperature had fallen below freezing.

Stepping up on wobbly cinder blocks, I hammered on the trailer's door.

"Coming, coming," said a voice. But a girl the age of the soccer player beat her mother to it. "Yes?" asked the woman. A cigarette hung from her mouth.

"Mrs. Kelly?"

"That's me."

Kelly was an auburn-haired woman in her thirties. She wore snug jeans and a sleeveless blouse over a small but attractive frame. That could not be said for the daughter. The poor girl had inherited her father's figure: practically no waistline and a rather plain face.

"You selling something, you've come to the wrong place." Kelly sucked off her cigarette, and then took the cigarette out of her mouth and let out a smoke-filled breath. "I'm a wage slave for Mister Milliken, my husband works for the Winn-Dixie, and if we had any damn money we wouldn't be living in a dump like this."

"Mrs. Kelly, the information I have is that your daughter was killed in this trailer park four years ago."

"Yes," she said with a nod. "The girl ran right out into the street. Never knew what hit her."

"And you had a baby-sitter?"

"It weren't Connie's fault, like I told people."

"Connie?" I asked, playing dumb.

"Connie Parnell. She was the girl sitting for my Terri. Young college girl who had dropped out of school because she became pregnant, then lost the baby and didn't want to go home. People tried to blame it on Connie, but it weren't her fault."

"Losing her baby?"

"No, no, my Terri. Never could control that girl." Kelly took another drag from her cigarette, inhaled deeply, then let out the smoke. "Never had any trouble with her sister here, but Terri, she were a handful."

"How old was Terri when she died?"

"Five."

"Connie Parnell was baby-sitting for you when Terri ran out into the street and was killed?" I wanted to be clear about what I was learning here. After all, Warden had given me this lead. Still, this woman's lack of sympathy was staggering.

"That's right." She took another drag off her cigarette and let the smoke out. It was enough to make me want a weed of my own, but since I was doing so well without them, I'd hang in there.

"Which trailer is Parnell's?"

Kelly shook her head. "You ain't gonna find her here. Connie moved out. Had to. People looking at her damn funny and there were no more baby-sitting jobs." Kelly glanced at her daughter. "Don't you talk like I'm talking to this lady here, you understand? That kind of talk is for adults and you ain't one yet."

The mother returned her attention to me. "Used to be able to take the kids over to her place anytime my old man and me wanted to go out and have a beer." Another drag on the cigarette, then, "You know, Connie had more education than she let on, but I don't think it was anything she could make a living at. When she told me she got pregnant and the baby died, well, it just knocked her for a loop. She hadn't recovered, then this happened."

Gone was any suspicion on this woman's part as to why I would be asking about her child's death. She was one of those women who loved to talk, and in her circle was probably known for being poor at keeping secrets.

"You don't know where I could find her, do you?"

"Have no idea. Connie just dropped off the face of the earth. I really hated that. Connie Parnell was the best baby-sitter I ever had."

11

"I need another name. I need something closer to the time when Megan disappeared."

I was in J.D. Warden's office with the big man and his partner. There had been no forwarding address for Connie Parnell at the trailer park in Spartanburg. So what else was new? Knowing this only frustrated me even more.

During the return trip to the Grand Strand, Chad and I had sat in rapt attention, listening to the radio account of the events occurring in Fort Smith. The backhoes had struck an unmarked water line and water had shot over fifty feet in the air. Before the rescue could continue, the line had to be cut off or capped.

"Do something!" screamed the child's mother on national TV and over the radio. The child's mom could see the water flowing toward the hole where her son was held prisoner. The report had shaken me so that Chad had to pull off to the side of the interstate and hold me. Megan was in the hands of a mad woman and I had no idea where she was.

"You've done a good job, Chase," Warden said. "Now leave it to the professionals."

"I can't. I'm too close."

"Being this close to a case is an even better reason for backing off."

"Susan . . . ."

Since Chad had returned to work, Mickey DeShields filled the sympathetic role in my quest. Mickey is one of the blackest men I have ever known. His skin almost has a blue hue to it. Mickey comes from money and dresses as he pleases: a high top-fade and clothes that look good only on him. Today his shirt and suit were light blue. A walking Picasso. Only his tie was different, pale. On him stuff like that looks phat. Or maybe I think Mickey looks good. He works out daily and no bad guy has ever outrun him.

"I know what you're going through," Mickey said. "When Christopher disappeared for a couple of hours, I was beside myself with worry."

I was close to tears but determined not to break down. Nothing had ever affected me this way. Dads said sooner or later I would have to admit to being a woman, and that my responsibilities as a woman were far greater than any man's. When Dads talks to me like a Dutch uncle, I know I've pressed him to the limits of his tolerance.

But this was my godchild and Megan didn't have anyone to take care of her. Hell, her grandparents didn't even know she was missing. Grandma and grandpa thought she was dead. But I knew better. I'd known from the moment that dirty diaper had been stuck in my face. Megan was alive!

I had to do something more than fidgeting around in this chair and listening to these two government agents drone on about how the authorities would handle everything in their own sweet time.

"You've gone as far as an amateur can go," Warden said. "It's up to the professionals to take it from here. We have the resources to track down this woman."

My mouth twisted into a frown. "That's so bogus I won't even comment."

"We came up with the woman in Spartanburg, didn't we?"

asked Warden, leaning back in his chair.

"That was over four years ago. No telling how many children have died since then."

"I've requested that the North Carolina State Bureau of Investigation put her name through their computer."

"What about Babe Parnell? Are they going to run her?"

"If you would give me a moment to finish . . . ." Warden stared at me. "Who the devil is Babe Parnell?"

"Connie Parnell's nickname."

He sat up. "Why didn't you say so?"

"I thought I did."

"And I thought we were making progress with you. If you had reports to write up, a nickname such as 'Babe' would've been in one of them."

"What are you talking about? I told you."

He waved me off as he reached for the phone.

Mickey and I sat there while Warden talked with someone named Bob Ferry. In a low voice, Mickey explained that Ferry was located in Columbia and ran the computer for SLED. Warden gave Ferry Connie Parnell's nickname.

I could not believe I had not told Warden Connie Parnell's nickname. The room spun and Mickey looked at me funny. Any moment one of my screws would come loose.

"Ferry will get back to me if he has a hit," said a voice out of a red fog.

"Susan, are you okay?" asked Mickey.

Warden hung up the phone. "Would you give us a moment, DeShields?"

"J.D., I'm not so sure this is the right time—"

"Let me take care of this . . . now."

Mickey nodded, stood up, and left the room.

"And close the door," added Warden.

DeShields did as asked and gave me a smile as he went out the door. I swallowed hard. I knew for a fact that I had told Warden everything I knew about Babe Parnell, exposed even more about myself.

143

Warden leaned forward on his desk. "Chase, would you agree you are a loose cannon?"

"I—I don't know about—"

"Just answer the question."

"Er—could I have a cigarette?"

"Absolutely not. You've been off them all week, so stay off them."

"How did you know . . . ?"

He waved this off. "You mentioned something about it when you first came in."

I didn't remember mentioning anything about my habit. "So I'm a loose cannon—what of it?"

"Still, wouldn't you agree you conducted yourself more professionally than in the past while investigating in Waxhaw, Rutledge College, and in that trailer park in Spartanburg?"

"I don't know . . . maybe." Where was all this going? I had to hit the road and find Megan.

"I know so. I didn't get any phone calls."

"But Chad said—"

"Yes—I got phone calls about your being rude, but people figured that had to do with your being concerned about your godchild. What I didn't get was calls about your drawing a gun, or chasing people through highly populated areas, or generally scaring hell out of people. Thankfully, not doing it naked."

I could've told him about Chad chasing me around the motel room while I was naked, but I didn't think that was what Warden had in mind or wanted to hear. I really didn't understand what he was getting at.

Warden glanced over my shoulder, then said, "Chase, admit it. With your boyfriend along, you acted differently than you would've if he hadn't, isn't that so?"

Warden was right. With those arms wrapped around me at night as I fell asleep . . . crying. "I guess so."

"It means there's hope for you yet."

"Hope?"

"My God, Chase, do I have to spell it out for you?"

"I guess you have to . . . ." What in the world did this have to do with Megan's disappearance?

Warden bit his lip. I'd never seen him so uptight. It was like a single dad having to explain the birds and the bees to his pubescent daughter.

"What I'm trying to say is I'm not the only one who has noticed the change. Harry Poinsett . . . ." He gestured at the door. "DeShields, too."

I turned around and saw several officers standing in the bullpen. Mickey was with them. All of them were staring in my direction.

Facing Warden, I asked, "What's up, J.D?"

Warden glanced at his watch, then got up and went to the glass door. He jerked it open. "DeShields, come in here, would you?"

Mickey glanced at the other officers who appeared to be a bit disappointed. Entering the office, Mickey was making a poor attempt not to smile.

Warden said, "I have to see the chief about something. Why don't you talk with Chase about that matter we discussed."

"Sure." Still smiling, Mickey took a seat at his own desk, which faced the wall. He swiveled around in his chair to face me. By now Warden was heading across the bullpen, almost at double-time. The cluster of cops broke up as he plowed through them.

"How far did he get, Susan?"

"I don't think we got anywhere. He was telling me I was a loose cannon, and that it was good Chad had been along or I would've gone off on someone." I glanced at the bullpen again. Warden was long gone. Maybe I should've cracked on him for insinuating that I had to have some guy along to mind my manners.

I fumbled around in my fanny pack. Along with the pack, I wore jeans, boots, a flannel shirt, and a down vest. If I was going to be on the street today, I wanted to be warm.

"I wouldn't smoke, Susan. Not today of all days."

"Well, you know about me and authority."

"And that's your problem. You won't knuckle under to anyone."

"Why should I?" I asked, tapping out a smoke.

"But we see a difference when you're with Rivers. You make compromises."

"Look," I said, still holding the cigarette, "I didn't come here to discuss what I have to do to keep my boyfriend happy. I came here for a lead on Connie Parnell. I'm going to find her, whether you and Warden help me or not."

"Then why haven't you lit up that cigarette? My telling you not to smoke has never stopped you before."

I glanced at the cigarette. "Mickey, would you just come out and say what's on your mind?"

"I'm not playing games, but I did win the pool."

"What in the world are you talking about?"

"I'm talking about Warden having trouble telling you what he has in mind. We had a pool on how long it would be before he gave up."

"Warden wants me to settle down. He wants me home, barefoot and pregnant. I didn't know you felt this way." Jeez, even Dads talked about it. Men think marriage or a good lay is the answer to every gal's problems. Well, a good lay, I couldn't argue with that.

DeShields was shaking his head. "If, and I'm saying if, Bob Ferry gets another hit on Connie Parnell, J.D.'s gotten approval from SLED for you to surveil Parnell to see if your godchild is with her."

"But he said it was time for the authorities to take over."

"He's testing you. To see if you'll follow his orders."

"Why for God's sake?"

"To see if there's a possibility you can work with SLED."

"Sorry, Mickey," I said, settling back into my chair. "I don't think I'm interested in doing the scut work while you get all the credit."

"I don't think SLED taking credit for your work was what J.D. had in mind."

It took a moment for the thought to connect, that's how far apart Warden and I were. "You mean he's trying to hire me?"

DeShields nodded. "And if this works out, he'll recommend you for the justice academy in Columbia."

I could only sit there, my mouth open. Now I needed something stronger than nicotine. This was totally beyond anything I expected. All those hints, the encouragement I'd received to go back to school—Warden was preparing me to come to work for SLED? I couldn't believe it and said so.

"Believe it, Susan, because it's true."

"But why couldn't he have told me himself? What's he afraid of?"

"That you'd turn him down."

"And why would I do that?"

"He never knows what to expect from you. You should see yourself. You don't look like you've been sleeping well. I tried to tell J.D. this wasn't the right time. But back to the job offer. Someone with a short fuse isn't the sort of person SLED is looking to hire."

"Who are they looking for?"

"You're a woman, street-tough, and experienced. It's frustrating when you hire a woman and she goes to pieces at her first confrontation. She has to be reassigned to the office and there are just so many clerks SLED needs."

"Get one from Charleston and you might get a black woman: a twofer."

"And that's what's worked before, but nobody wants to work at the beach."

"You've got to be kidding. I love it here."

"You might, but Myrtle Beach is on the fast track to nowhere. I've been here six years and I don't think I'll ever catch up with the guys in my class at the academy."

"At least you've got the beach."

"And that's why I don't give a damn if I make lieutenant or not. Think it over, Susan. There's going to be a slot opening up. Plenty of work, too, with the Grand Strand growing. And the brass running SLED would love to hire someone for a district office who's not looking to come to Columbia and take their job."

"I'd have to go back to school, wouldn't I?"

"At least have your GED, maybe take some courses at the local tech school."

"And act more responsibly."

"There's that."

"It also means I should go home and forget about Megan."

"I don't think you can ever forget such a tragedy, but a time-out might provide you with a much-needed rest. We'll call you with any leads. You don't have any leads, do you?"

I shook my head. "Nothing, and I'm being straight with you. I don't know what to do next."

"Then go home and rest. Believe me, Susan, you look like you need it."

"I—I can't."

"Susan, this is your big chance."

"I know, I know, but that baby abandoned along the Natchez Trace was still alive. Missing for whole a week but found alive when Warden inquired with the authorities in Mississippi. I think Parnell had that baby, then told the authorities where to find her."

"Why would she do that?"

"To show people she could take care of a child. Or prove it to herself."

"That's a bit far-fetched, don't you think?"

"I talked with Deitz last night. She's the shrink at Rutledge College who's helping Louise Moultrie work her way through the death of her child. Deitz said she's had time to consider what she and I talked about, that the kidnapping of my godchild would be another step in Parnell's rehabilitation."

"I don't propose to understand a thing you've said, but

yes, SLED wants you to drop this until we have a firm lead."

"Sorry, Mickey, but if you know anything about me, you know I can't take a time-out, knowing Megan's out there . . . somewhere."

"But if Parnell returned the child to the parents along the Natchez Trace, why wouldn't she do the same with Megan Destefani?"

"Simple, Mickey," I said, getting to my feet. "Because no one's looking for Megan."

12

Though I waited around the law enforcement center for another hour, nothing came through from Columbia. I smoked and joked with the cops outside the building where us smokers spend our purgatory, especially during cold winters and hot summers. All the time I wondered if I could fit in with these guys. They seemed like regular people, but I'd be working for the South Carolina Law Enforcement Division, and the attitude of local cops toward SLED is the same as SLED's attitude when the *feebs* muscle in on their territory.

The local cops would remember me from chasing the naked girl through the lobby of the Host of Kings' Hotel and the kid who leaped to his death from the Garden City pier when I was actually after his girlfriend. I'd tried to save the boy, but the dumb-ass was lost in a mean riptide we were having that season. Truth was, if someone hadn't tossed me a rope, I might have joined him.

But to be a real cop . . . now that was something I'd never dreamed of. I mean, for someone who'd scuffled for a living ever since she'd been fifteen. Marvin wouldn't like it. He could call on me to lifeguard anytime, if I didn't have business elsewhere. Standing there smoking and joking, I remembered

I did have business elsewhere, and I left the law enforcement center with no more than a cursory nod to Warden as we passed in the hall.

Instead of returning to Wacca Wache Landing, I drove to the Pirate's Cove. With the key Donna had given me, I let myself into the empty apartment.

I strolled through the living room, where Chad and I had made love in front of the fireplace, and passed a dead phone clinging to the wall. I shuddered. When you die, there's no one to take your phone to your next destination. I pulled my vest in close to my body. The place could use a little heat. It was cold in here.

Walking down the hall, I told myself to get a grip. Then I turned the corner and stepped into what had been my godchild's bedroom, a room I'd helped decorate.

Donna and I thought we could improve on the off-white walls, and we had, changing the baby's room to a rosy pink color. The resident manager learned what we'd done and reminded Donna that the room would have to be repainted off-white before she moved out.

What did it matter if the walls were pink or purple? Painters were going to repaint the whole damn place whenever Donna moved out. The border we had done in Winnie the Pooh, Piglet, Eeyore, Rabbit, and Tigger, too. Tears formed in my eyes. Winnie the Pooh blankets, sheets, bedcovers and curtains, even a mobile Megan would lay under, cooing . . . .

I began to sob, sliding down the wall and leaning into it.

From the door came, "You're not going to faint again, are you?"

I rolled away, over the lump that was my fanny pack. When I came to a stop, the gun came out and I sighted down the barrel . . . and saw the painter in the doorway. He was still the tall, lean guy with off-white freckles spotting his face, his jeans and an old pair of running shoes.

"Damn!" he shouted, stepping back into the hall.

Shit. This wasn't anything close to acting responsibly. I stood up and put away my gun. "Sorry. You startled me."

He wiped his forehead with a paint-smeared sleeve. "I was only asking . . . I was only asking if you were about to faint. Damn, lady, where'd that gun come from?"

"My purse," I said, velcroing the Smith & Wesson back into my fanny pack.

"I've never . . . I've never seen a gun come out so fast." His Adam's apple bobbed. "Even on TV."

"Don't worry about it," I said, crossing the room to the door. "It was my fault. I shouldn't've come back." Brushing away a tear, I added, "This place brings back memories. I was reliving them when you startled me."

"This the room of the baby who disappeared during the storm?"

I nodded.

"Ever find her?"

"SLED is . . . SLED and I are working on it, but we've run out of leads. I thought I might be inspired by returning to the scene. Bad idea." I handed him the key. "This belongs to the complex."

He took the key. "Wish you luck, ma'am. Maybe it'll work out like it did for that kid in Arkansas. That tunnel rat from Vietnam, he was right when he said he could get that boy out of that hole. All that machinery standing around and this guy just slips down into that hole. Sure, they had to grease him down with axle grease and tie a rope around his feet, but he got that kid outta there."

"Only after the mother pleaded with the authorities to give him a chance."

"Well, the water, it was rising. I don't think they thought the backhoes were going to reach the kid soon enough. I kept the radio on the whole time. Better than any ball game." He scanned the room. "Well, got to get started. Her folks, meaning the woman who died, were here yesterday moving her things out. Place was free a week ago, but her father couldn't get here to pick it up. Something about the wife being sick."

"She has Alzheimer's."

He nodded. "All these units have to be ready by spring. Seems like people arrive at the beach earlier and earlier these days." He scanned the room. "It's all the articles in magazines my boss told me, like that lady you're looking for. She wrote some of them articles, bringing people down here." Now he was staring at the Winnie the Pooh border that ran around the room. He fished a knife out of his jeans. "This border's not supposed to be here. I'll have to take it down and they'll charge it against the security deposit."

"I don't think Donna's family will mind." I wiped away a tear. "Er—what were you saying about articles in magazines?"

The painter stopped trying to lift off the border with his knife. "My boss said tourism is the second leading industry in the state, and I'm beginning to believe him. The way people pour into the Grand Strand, I reckon this side of the state will get so heavy, one day it'll just slide off in the ocean."

Connie Parnell had been here to do an article on the Grand Strand. That's why she was here in the dead of winter. The article was to come out in the spring, when folks were making their plans for the beach. Babe had said something about working several months ahead, that most magazines accepted Christmas articles during the summer, vice versa for summer articles. I'd only looked for writers with the same last name. I'd try again, but this time I'd be more specific. I'd keep a record of the names of anyone who had done articles on the Natchez Trace and any other areas Connie Parnell had mentioned.

I've found the library to be a good place to think. You might think I could walk the beach and sort things out, but being a lifeguard, you can't keep your eyes off the water.

Jenny Rogers had returned to work in the reference department, her stint at self-exploration as an artist not having worked out. I, however, was looking forward to working for SLED and it probably showed on my face. Jenny seemed embarrassed as she greeted me from behind the counter. After all, I had had to track her down. Jenny still had long brown hair to her shoulders, wore a dress with few frills or color, granny glasses, and absolutely no makeup. Jenny could've been a prettier girl. Big doe eyes she could've built a wardrobe or a life around if she'd wanted to. People wanted to take care of Jenny Rogers. Now those doe eyes stared at the floor.

"How's your mom, Jenny?"

"She's—she's just fine. I couldn't leave her in that house alone."

"You did the right thing," I said with a cheery smile. I wasn't going to do anything to screw up my opportunity with SLED.

Now those brown eyes looked at me. "I'm glad you think so."

"Jenny, I need your help, and I'm going to need one of your computers that connects to the Internet."

"Oh, goody, I always liked helping you with your cases, the few times you asked."

"Those times might even be less. I may be going to work for SLED."

"How exciting. I'm sure that's something you've always wanted to do: be a real private detective."

Instead of telling this woman I always thought I'd been a real private eye, that's why SLED was interested in hiring me, I said, "Let me tell you what's up." Jeez, but Warden really knew my hot button.

I was compiling a list of people who'd written articles about the southeastern United States when Louise Moultrie threw her coat over a chair at the long table where I was working.

"Having any luck?"

I could only stare. The heavy woman wore a forest green

sweat suit in the Rutledge College colors, not the usual preppy stuff.

"Surprised to see me?" she asked, hanging a bag-like purse on the back of another chair.

"Er—yes, Dean."

"I'm not a dean today. I took a leave of absence."

"For what?"

"To help you locate Connie Parnell."

"Doctor Deitz isn't going to like that." Besides, I was solving this case on my own and getting that job at SLED.

"Screw Deitz. I'm going to find Connie Parnell even if I have to do it on my own time." She pulled a chair from under the table and sat down. "And you're to call me 'Louise' while we're working together."

"I don't know if that's a good idea or not, Dean—er, Louise."

"And why's that?" She pulled out her cigarettes. "They let you smoke in here?"

"You have to go outside." First my boyfriend tagging along, now this woman. All she'd do was get in my way.

Moultrie returned the cigarettes to her purse and took out a pack of gum. She offered me a stick. "Didn't smoke for the longest, but this has upset me so . . . ." When I declined her offer, she popped the gum into her mouth.

"I don't think this is going to work—us working together."

She leaned back, eyeing me. "You seemed fairly keen on finding Connie when you came to see me. Nothing's changed, has it? You still want to locate your godchild, don't you?"

"I do."

"And I want to bring Connie Parnell to justice, so I don't see the problem. I'll pay my own way."

"I don't like people looking over my shoulder. When my boyfriend was along I liked it even less." Well, part of that was true.

"What are you saying—that he was a distraction?"

"Exactly."

"Fine," she said, putting a hand on my shoulder. "Then

I'll make it my job to focus you on your work."

"I don't see how you can."

"Because, my dear, it is my job, every single day, to focus young people on their work." She let go of my shoulder. "You may not know this, but the two most important people at any institution of higher learning are the one who keeps the grade point average up, which draws the right students, and the person who brings the money in, no explanation needed. The president, if she has any sense, stays out of their way and lets them do their jobs."

"I don't think I could've cut it at Rutledge."

"I disagree. Your lack of formal education shouldn't be a barrier in returning to school. You have the qualities that schools are looking for: intelligence, initiative, and a decent work ethic." She gestured at the stacks of microfilm and legal pads on the table. "That's demonstrated by what you're doing. I was immediately attracted to you because I saw you as one of our graduates, working in the real world. Organized, purposeful, and respectful but not taking any crap off anyone. I talked with Deitz." Moultrie smiled. "Ollie didn't like your approach, threatening to stay involved in my life until the issue of Connie Parnell was resolved. But it scored points with me. The only thing I didn't understand was why you brought along your boyfriend. You certainly didn't need him."

"We were working out an unrelated issue."

"And did you?"

"I don't see that's any of your business."

"It's not. I only wanted to know if he's going to be a distraction."

"No one's going to distract me, Dean, not even you."

"'Louise,' please, but the bottom line is, I won't be a distraction." She smiled. "You see, you tried to get me off the subject—"

"Which is?"

"The fact I will not distract you."

I had to smile. This woman was good and it was evident she wasn't going away.

"Susan, I'm not your boyfriend, I'm not your boss, and I'm certainly not the enemy, but I am going to keep you focused. I don't have my whole life to devote to finding Connie Parnell, just a couple of weeks. I'm also here because, since you spent time with Parnell, it's possible you might know something that could help us find her. I've used three different detective agencies and all they've done is made me persona non grata in Waxhaw."

I chuckled. "No wonder they gave me such a hard time."

"Of course. Plenty of my people had been through that town before you arrived."

I gestured at the magazines and computer printouts on the table. "I'm trying to get a sense of where the woman's been and the one place she might be."

"Okay, let's get down to business."

I couldn't help but like this woman. She was the kind of person you hoped your mother would be when you wanted more than a hug and fresh-baked cookies. "What did you have in mind?"

She pulled a folder from her huge purse. "This is everything I have in my files about Connie." The folder overflowed with newspaper clippings and transcripts, reports by private investigators who had followed up every lead. "I know Deitz would think this was unhealthy, keeping a file about Connie—"

"Obsessing."

"Much like you've done with your godchild."

"Touché."

"And I might suggest this game-playing is also a distraction."

"Agreed."

"Fact is, this file was stored in the attic where I never see it. I did the same with all of my daughter's things. I put them away. I kept one of her photographs—Katherine's best,

I think. I didn't turn her room into a shrine." She stopped to dab at her eyes with a Kleenex. "But this, too, is another distraction from what we're trying to accomplish."

I patted her arm. "Not at all. I think having Chad around made me fight for Megan even more, and that was good. Now I don't need a devil's advocate, I need some heavy duty support."

She pushed her file at me. "Then why don't you read what I've got and I'll read what you've got, then we'll put our heads together over dinner. My treat."

"I can pay my way."

"And you will, my dear," she added with a smile, "until it becomes a distraction."

13

After registering Louise at a motel near the landing—
Louise had flown into Myrtle Beach—I took her to Captain Jack's for a seafood dinner. Captain Jack's is one of
those places off the beaten path that only the locals know
about. The food is delicious and the prices reasonable. Louise
was like a little kid, even to the point of making me share
pieces from her plate I already knew tasted better than anything she'd find inland. We were like mother and daughter,
as when Louise would draw me up short.

"Now not too much wine, Susan. We need to be able to
concentrate."

"Wine's no problem. It's the hard stuff that gets me." And
why I'd drunk so much after Megan and her mother had
died. Died? Disappeared! I excused myself and rushed into
the rest room.

When I returned my face wasn't as warm, still, I sipped
from a glass of iced tea ordered especially for me. "Where do
we begin?"

"Anywhere you'd like," said my new friend, not comment-
ing on my long disappearance. "I rather think it's like free
association."

Hmm. That was not how I would usually proceed. Using a paid database, I had located a Kathy Strickland who worked at *The Lost Colony*. And that name had been on many articles written about the history of the American southeast. We should be on our way to Manteo, but Louise demurred. *The Lost Colony* wasn't open this time of year, she said. It should be one of many destinations on our list. We shouldn't go charging off in any particular direction until we agreed on the locales with the highest probability. She was right, and I was trying to be more responsible. Besides, Louise was fun to be around, and not at all like the losers J.D. Warden accused me of usually hanging with.

I said, "The problem with 'Connie Parnell' is that after Spartanburg, she disappeared."

"Until she reappeared in Myrtle Beach four years later. I wonder what that means, and using her real name, too."

"Maybe she thought she was cured after the safe return of the baby on the Natchez Trace?"

Moultrie shrugged. "Makes as much sense as anything else. But why hasn't anyone been able to locate her?"

"Because there's no driver's license, no social security number, or arrest record for Connie Parnell." I gestured inland. "She's out there somewhere, hovering under the radar." Raising my hand had stirred my stomach.

"And the Internet?"

"There is no 'Connie Parnell' byline. There are plenty of names, like the one who did the articles for the Smithsonian about the Natchez Trace, but that was a different name, a different social security number—"

"Where does she get these numbers?"

"She probably buys old hard drives when people upgrade their computers," I said, trying to ignore my stomach. "People forget they've put their personal history on those hard drives. Once she has access to the bogus information, anything on an arrest record—"

"Is also bogus?"

I nodded. "The problem you have with someone who's childless . . . ." I stopped, realizing what I'd just said, and what it meant to the woman across the table from me. "The problem you have with someone who is constantly on the move is that self-employed individuals don't leave much of a trail. No trail at all if they don't care to be found." Scooting back in my chair to give myself some air, I went on to add that no "Connie Parnell" or "Babe Parnell" had been in a car wreck, robbed a bank, or even received a traffic ticket. SLED had access to those records, but they'd come up empty.

My stomach was turning over again. I might have to make a return visit to the rest room.

". . . thought that Parnell was reaching out to you, trying to leave you a message how to find her."

"What? Oh, yes . . . I think she was."

"Then start with when you met her. How did you feel when you two first met?"

"I didn't like her."

"Why?"

"She was way weird."

"What exactly didn't ring true?"

"Parnell said things aren't always as they appear."

"No kidding," said Louise with a laugh. "I think that comes with growing up."

"No. Not the real world. Parnell focused on what wasn't so, not what people thought to be true." I shook my head. "I'm not getting this right."

"Take your time."

Between Louise's plate and mine, I'd eaten too much. That's what was wrong. Damn visitors from out of town. They always do that, make you eat too much, stay out too late, and get you out of your rhythm.

Who was I to complain? When was the last time I'd had visitors from out of town? I asked the waitress for a Coke. Perhaps a soda would settle my stomach and I could start enjoying the evening with my new friend.

After the drink arrived and I'd taken a swallow, I said, "People think I'm cynical, but Connie seemed to relish . . . the dark side of life." I burped—a big fat juicy one. "Sorry. That was the Coke talking. Anyway, Babe was always going on about what fools people were to believe what we were told by the news media and what we read in history books."

"For instance?"

"That Saturday afternoon I spent with her, one of the lists of the scientists and doctors of the last century flashed on ED-TV. The list featured the people who had made it possible for us to live longer—the inventor of penicillin, the polio vaccine—you know the kind of list. It was all the rage at the end of the millennium. Babe just laughed at the TV and said 'bullshit. It was clean water.' You see what I mean?"

Moultrie nodded. "I remember that cocksureness. Once I was cornered at a mixer by Connie. She went on and on about Woodrow Wilson and how he was influenced by his wife's circle and those people were Southerners. By the end of Wilson's administration, the federal government was completely segregated, worse than before the Civil War. She said that Mrs. Wilson called black people 'darkies.' It wasn't as bad as the n-word, but Connie's point was that people in this country shouldn't have revered Wilson as a champion of human rights."

I nodded in agreement. "Mine was Helen Keller. Babe went on and on about how Keller was a socialist and wobbled in politics—"

"A Wobbly?"

"That's it. Keller was against one of the world wars, I don't remember which one. People had said Helen Keller was so bright when she learned to communicate, you know, the stuff in the movies with her hand under the water faucet. When Keller turned against the world war, people said what could she know, this deaf and blind woman?" My stomach-ache had returned with a vengeance. "If I didn't know any better, I'd think I was going to be sick."

"Too much wine," said my new friend with a chuckle. "Why don't you go to the bathroom and see what happens."

"Yes, Mother."

"Susan, I didn't mean—"

"No, no," I said, struggling out of my chair. "You're right. I'll go."

When I returned to the table, and after nothing had happened in the toilet, I found another Coke waiting. "I don't think I want another one of those." The condition of my stomach had not changed. It remained unsettled.

"Captain Jack said they're closing, but we could stay a little longer if we need to. Maybe we should be getting on if you're not feeling well."

"I'm okay if you are."

"Then let's return to Connie or Kathy or whatever she called herself." Moultrie was chewing a piece of gum instead of having a cigarette.

"Well, I knew her as Babe and that afternoon I spent with her, she said we didn't kill off the Indians like we see in the movies. That when the Pilgrims landed they were able to take over because of the plague."

"The plague?"

"The one that killed all those people in Europe."

"I don't understand. What did the Black Death have to do with North America?"

"According to Babe, it got loose over here and wiped out the Indians. The Indians who were left, the ones who helped the Pilgrims, welcomed them with open arms because there wasn't anyone to live in all the empty villages."

"It doesn't sound like what I've read about the first Thanksgiving. What else did she say?"

"That no one would publish those kinds of articles."

"She could've tried a scholarly journal, if she had research to back it up."

"She'd never do that because journals don't pay diddly. She might be right. I didn't see Parnell's name listed in any of the journals I checked."

My stomach did not feel well at all. It must've been something I ate. Now that would tick off Captain Jack. And disappoint Louise. She was so excited about eating here and I'd gotten a bad piece of fish.

"What else, Susan?"

Jeez! When this woman said she was going to keep me focused, she hadn't been kidding.

"Oh, Babe went on about how we wiped out the Indians with the plague, drove them out of their homelands, and finally onto those reservations."

"But that wouldn't have anything to do with the southeastern United States, and if she's gone out west to prove some cockeyed theory, we don't stand a chance of finding her. No. We have to concentrate on this part of the country."

I was cramping up and it wasn't even that time of month. Could I be pregnant? Impossible. Chad always used protection. "I'm sticking with my theory that she's somewhere she's never written about, a place she wouldn't want to draw attention to. Her . . . nest." Tears came to my eyes as I clutched my stomach. "Warden . . . Warden called Manteo and told the police chief about Parnell. The chief said . . . ."

"Susan, you don't look so good."

"I don't feel so good." At the moment I was leaning over, practically clutching my stomach. I felt cold and hot at the same time. Could I be having an attack of appendicitis?

"Let's get you home. Will you let me drive your jeep?"

Struggling to my feet, I said, "I don't think I have any choice."

Captain Jack was at the register when Louise paid the check. She paid in cash and I didn't argue. It was all I could do to stand, and believe me, it wasn't very straight. Maybe I should return to the rest room and jam a finger down my throat.

Jack was a short fellow with a ring of hair around his head and a potbelly stomach. The title of "captain" was honorary. As far as I knew, Jack had never skippered any craft. "Susan, did you drink too much again?"

"I'm driving her home," volunteered Moultrie.

"Good. Susan doesn't need to be picked up by the police again."

Louise stared at me. Jeez, as if having an upset stomach wasn't enough.

Down the road, I had to have Louise pull over so I could puke. It gave me no relief. I had a tremendous pain in my gut, and before we were halfway back to the motel, I was doubled up.

"Susan, are you all right?"

"I . . . feel like shit." Waves of hot and cold rushed through me. It was the worst case of the flu I'd ever had.

"You need to see a doctor."

"No, no . . . ."

"If you can't sit up, I'm taking you to a hospital."

I couldn't sit up, I couldn't stand, I couldn't move, so I ended up at the emergency room on a gurney, in the fetal position. Someone asked questions and Louise filled them in. She said it had to be food poisoning, but that couldn't be right. Louise wasn't sick and I'd eaten off her plate.

A doctor came into the curtained-off area. I told him I thought I was having an attack of appendicitis.

"Let me make the medical evaluations, young lady." He glanced at Louise. "This your mother?"

"A . . . friend."

"Then she will have to wait outside."

"Let her stay. I'm an orphan." I didn't know why I said that, but Louise was so easy to open up to, and there was so much pain. I gripped my tummy and moaned.

The doctor began to poke and probe and make me feel even worse. It was hard to keep straightened out. The pain in my stomach kept me doubled over. The few times I opened my eyes and saw Louise through my tears, she was chewing her lip and I was holding her hand. It was good to have a friend at a time like this.

In the end, the doctor's diagnosis was the same as Louise's: food poisoning. They would pump my stomach, then stash me in a room overnight. Louise said she would stay with me, and she did, until I passed out.

When I woke up, Chad was sitting by my bed. Sunlight streamed through the window, but it looked fuzzy, not sharp in color.

"How you feeling, Suze?"

"Better than last night."

"Uh-huh. Minute I leave you, look what happens."

I looked around. "Where's Louise?"

He slid to the edge of his chair. "Dean Moultrie from Rutledge College?"

"Yes."

"She's not here. Why would she be?"

"We were working . . . ." I had to stop to gather my thoughts. "We were working on the Parnell case."

"Why would you do that? That woman's every bit as much a fruitcake as Parnell."

"She's my friend."

"Look, I don't know what you're talking about, but Louise Moultrie is not here. I was called by the hospital. Dads is out of town and my name was on the people-to-contact-in-case-of-emergency in your wallet. Are you sure you're okay? They told me you ate something that disagreed with you."

"At Captain Jack's."

"You're kidding."

"Louise and I went there last night. She's staying at the Blackbeard Motel."

Chad still didn't believe me so I had him call. When he returned to the room, he said, "There's no one staying there by that name."

"Then she's already checked out." I sat up and looked

around for my clothes. I was wearing one of those stupid hospital gowns that opens in the back and allows your ass to flap in the breeze.

"What I mean, Suze, is she was never there."

"That's not true. I saw her go inside and register."

"Then she didn't register under that name. There is no Louise Moultrie there."

"She used another name?"

"And why would she do that?"

"You said she was a fruitcake."

Chad didn't know what to say to that.

"Do me a favor, would you? Call them again and describe the woman. She wore a green sweatshirt under a heavy coat."

"Dean Moultrie in sweats. You really do need to get some rest."

When Chad returned, I was pulling on my pants and using the edge of the bed to keep my balance.

Chad rushed over and grabbed my arm. "What are you doing?"

"Heading to North Carolina."

"Why?"

"To find the Lost Colony."

"If it's been lost this long, it won't matter if it stays lost a few more days."

"What did you learn at the Blackbeard Motel?"

"A woman stopped there yesterday and wrote down some rates, but she didn't take a room. The desk clerk remembered because the woman arrived in a jeep with a footlocker welded where the backseat should be. I knew whose jeep that was, so I went downstairs and talked with the people in the emergency room. They said a woman matching Louise Moultrie's description was with you last night. She talked so long on her cell phone that the battery went dead and she had to switch to a pay phone in the hall. Suze, what's going on?"

"I'll explain on the way to North Carolina."

14

It was late afternoon when we arrived at the Outer Banks. I slept most of the way. Chad goosed the 'vette, really stepping on it. I'd never seen him drive so fast, radar detectors forward and aft, tinfoil in the hubcaps; we were really blowing down the road. Chad requisitioned a blanket and pillow from the hospital and bundled me up in the passenger seat. Our only stop was a Circle K where he boiled some oatmeal and made me eat it.

"You're not going to be able to stay on your feet when we get to Manteo unless you eat," he had said.

I continued to sip Gatorade as he drove across the bridge into Manteo, your typical waterfront town. If I'd been in the touristy mood, Chad and I could've strolled hand in hand along its waterfront, or taken a tour of the *Elizabeth II* moored there. Think of something along the lines of the *Mayflower.* Manteo has tree-lined streets named for characters from *The Lost Colony.* Its downtown is full of quaint shops and places to fill your stomach with fresh seafood.

Ugh!

Of course, why was I blaming seafood? Louise Moultrie had slipped me some kind of Roofie.

As we rolled into town I heard myself say, "I'll go to counseling, if that's what you want."

Chad glanced at me. "I don't want you to go unless you see a need."

"I do."

"You don't sound very happy about it."

"I'm supposed to enjoy discussing my mental health with some shrink who'll confirm what people already know?"

"I only meant—"

"I know what you meant!" I took a final sip of my Gatorade and twisted the cap back on the bottle. "But I'm not going with you."

Chad was watching me more than the road. When I reminded him of this, he returned the 'vette to our side of the yellow line.

"Chad, I've seen plenty of my friends die from drinking, drugs, sex, or just plain recklessness. I refused to be sucked under. It's not like people think. I never had a chip on my shoulder." Looking at the streets with their manicured lawns, picket fences, and tastefully decorated houses, I added, "Warden thinks I hang with weirdos so I don't have to let anyone in, but that's not true either."

"It's not?"

I felt a flash of anger about Chad's discussing me with J.D. Warden, but I reminded myself that he and Warden were genuinely concerned about me. "How the devil am I supposed to relate to people like you?"

His hand was back, trying to find mine. I pulled away and saw the reaction on his face, not anger but puzzlement.

"You just don't get it, do you?" I asked.

"No—I don't."

"You want me to be a Yuppie. That's why I need counseling—to fit into your world."

"Suze, I'm not asking you to change."

"I have to." Now my hand was clutching his. "You have what I want. I mean, you're what I want. And that's why I'll go see the shrink myself."

"And you don't want quid pro quo?"

"I just want an opportunity to straighten out my life."

"Does that include marrying me some day?"

"Maybe. Once I straighten myself out."

The chief of police was a skinny man, about fifty. He wore a uniform that appeared to have been purchased before he'd gone on his latest diet: navy blue pants with a light blue blouse and a string tie that looked like something one of the locals would've made, perhaps even an Indian. The nameplate on his desk read: Happy Largo. He was bald, but hair stuck out of the front of his shirt and ran down his forearms.

The chief looked up from reading a manual as Chad opened the door for me. The manual explained how to operate a fax machine. The machine and the box sat on the desk in front of him. From the cell block came singing that was out of tune.

He put down the instructions. "What can I do for you, young man?"

Since I was about to become a different person, I didn't punch out the chief for disrespecting me but allowed my boyfriend to say, "We're looking for a missing person, Chief. Her name is Connie Parnell. She goes by the nickname of 'Babe.'"

The chief gave me a glance, then returned his attention to my boyfriend. "Missing from where, son?"

"From Waxhaw. She also travels under the name of Constance Delphine Parnell."

The dispatcher put down her romance novel. It was the first time I'd noticed the woman sitting in the corner at a table in front of a bunch of radio gear. She said, "Chief, that's the one come over the wire from South Carolina."

"Do you have some ID, young fellow?"

Chad looked at me as I opened my purse and handed over my PI identification. The chief compared the ID photograph to me, though I'm sure I was a lot paler since having my stomach pumped.

"Says here you're licensed as a private investigator in the state of South Carolina, Miss Chase."

"Yes, sir, and by rule I must report to you when I arrive in town."

"That's correct." He returned the ID. "And you, young fellow? Who are you?"

"Just the driver. Susan was sick but wanted to wrap this up."

"Well, young lady, I don't want to tell you your business . . . ."

Which meant he was about to.

"But if you want any law enforcement officer to take you seriously, you can't have your boyfriend doing all the talking, whether you've got an upset stomach or not." He gave me a look that said he knew my problems were women's problems and to stop whining and get on with the job.

"I'll keep that in mind, Chief."

We took seats in chairs in front of the desk. When I had finished my tale, the chief asked to see a picture of the Parnell woman, the one I carried everywhere and showed to everyone. Chad had to pass it over. I was spent.

"You think your godchild is with this woman?"

"Yes, sir."

The dispatcher came over and stood behind the chief to look at the photo. The dispatcher was a big woman, tall as me. In her hand was a sheet of paper.

"This what you're looking for, Happy?" It was the APB issued by SLED. "I told you this favored Kathy Strickland, just the wrong color hair."

Kathy Strickland was one of the names I'd come up with on the paid database. Still, it was all I could do to sit up straight.

Chad asked, "Who's that?"

"Local girl," said the chief.

"She's no local," said the dispatcher. "I don't reckon

Kathy's been here more than four years."

I gathered up the energy to ask, "Where can I find this woman? The name is an alias the Parnell woman uses."

"Miss Chase, we don't know for sure that Kathy's the one you're looking for."

It's a bad sign when the cops refer to a local by his or her first name. "Does she have a child with her?"

"Around these parts we don't mess in people's business. We leave them pretty much alone."

"Chief, I don't know how to put this, but if my godchild is harmed in any way since . . ." I glanced at my watch and told him the time, ". . . I will hold you and the city of Manteo responsible." Hell, if Myrtle Beach could hold me responsible for that doper leaping to his death when I was after his girlfriend, I could sue these people's asses. I collapsed back in my chair, arms limp on the wraparound armrests.

"Yeah. That's her," said the dispatcher from behind the chief.

"Gloria, don't you have something to do?"

"Not that much during the off-season, Happy."

"Miss Chase, threats aren't going to get you any cooperation from this office."

"Chief, everywhere I go people are always giving this Parnell woman the benefit of the doubt and yet children continue to die. I apologize if I come across as rude, but I've been beside myself with worry." I let my level gaze drop to the floor.

"Well, I've been the chief of police of this town for more than twenty years and I've seen more than I care to when it comes to human suffering. I don't want you barging into Kathy's life without any warning."

Looking up, I said, "After just getting out of the hospital, I can promise you that I won't be barging in anywhere."

Largo pushed back from his desk. "I'll go with you and your friend. I wouldn't want Kathy to think we were ganging up on her."

We weren't. This was between Babe, or Connie, or Kathy, and me. Weak as a kitten, I still liked the odds.

"I'd be surprised if she's in town," said the dispatcher from where she had retaken her seat at the table in front of the radio gear.

"Why do you say that?" I asked, using the arms of the chair to help me stand.

"It's the off-season and that's when Kathy does her traveling. Kathy has family all over. They put her up because she don't have no regular job during the off-season. She baby-sits for them."

A tremor ran through me. Chad saw this and gripped my arm.

"Kathy only works when the colony's in session. She's what you'd call permanent part-time."

"The colony?" asked Chad.

"*The Lost Colony,*" explained the chief. "It's a play put on each summer to commemorate the first white colony to be founded in America."

"Babe Parnell is in that?"

"I don't know nothing about this Parnell woman, but Kathy Strickland's been working for *The Lost Colony* the last three or four years. And she's got longer hair than what was in that picture and it's blond."

My heart was in my throat. "Does she have a baby with her?" I repeated.

"Sometimes, during the off-season."

"What are you talking about, sometimes? People don't just have babies and get rid of them." I could feel myself trembling. Chad put an arm around my back, grasping me at the waist, holding me on my feet.

"Kathy can't have children of her own," said the chief. "She was married once, but it didn't take."

"When the guy learned she was barren," said the dispatcher from her table. "Least that's what Kathy told us. Occasionally, she'll have one of her nieces or nephews here for a week or two but always before the Season starts. She shows that baby around town just like it was her own. Happy, I told you there was something strange about that woman, folks allowing their babies to be taken away for weeks at a time."

"Gloria, you're always looking for trouble where there's none. Maybe if you had to handle a few of these domestics it'd slow you down."

"Just waiting to be made a real deputy. You know I passed all the courses the city requires."

"Take it up with the city council. They're the ones who give me a budget to work with."

Outside, the chief got into a blue-and-white patrol car. Chad opened the door of the Corvette and I climbed inside. Tears were already rolling down my cheeks. I shook. When Chad got in from his side, he put his arm around me.

"Don't worry, Suze. Everything will be all right."

I sniffed, wiped my tears away, and sat up. In front of us the cruiser moved out.

According to the chief, Connie Parnell or Kathy Strickland, or whoever the hell this woman was, rented an apartment two blocks off the ocean. The owner lived downstairs and rented out the top floor. And Kathy Strickland had never been in trouble with the law.

"Good girl. God-fearing," said the chief as we stepped inside a hedge separating the sidewalk from the postage-stamp yard of the house where Strickland lived. "Attends the same church as my family." He headed up the sidewalk leading to the house, then preceded us onto the porch where he rang the bell. "Kathy hung around *The Lost Colony* helping out until they finally asked her to be part of the ensemble. We call them stage groupies, and a good number of them are asked to stay on. *The Lost Colony* runs the new hires through me, and Kathy Strickland checked out. I don't rightly remember where she was from, but best I remember, it was somewhere near Charlotte."

"People in this town aren't going to be happy to learn they've been sheltering a baby killer."

"Now, now, Miss Chase, I know you've been under a great deal of strain, but let's not overreact. We're not sure Kathy Strickland's the person SLED is looking for."

"Then why's that guy in the Ford parked down the street?" I gestured with my head, keeping my hands in my pockets. "He must be freezing his ass off without having his heater running."

The chief returned to the edge of the porch and looked down the street. As we watched, the sedan came to life, left its parking space, and moved to the corner, where it turned inland.

"Who was that, Suze?"

"One of Louise Moultrie's private eyes, I would imagine."

"She employs more than one?"

"That's who she was on the phone with at the hospital. They've been in town since morning knocking on doors and flashing badges and asking 'Have you seen this young lady?'" I gripped Chad's arm so to stay on my feet. I was running low on gas. "I've done it . . . before. Wear your badge where people can see it . . . don't talk much. Like a cop."

The chief was staring at me.

"When the private investigators reported they had a fix on someone who might be Connie Parnell, Moultrie left the hospital and drove up here." I looked at the chief, who had taken off his cap and was scratching his head.

"Probably some salesman checking his bearings," he said, putting his hat back on. "Had to be." He tried the bell again, then said, "I'll check upstairs."

"Strickland won't be up there or Louise Moultrie would be here."

Still he climbed the wooden stairs on the outside of the house while Chad and I watched from the driveway. I had to conserve my energy. I might need it. God, but did I hope I'd need it. Chad held me upright as the wind bore down on us.

175

I turned my back to the ocean, but the wind still cut through me like a knife. Or perhaps that was fear.

A two-car garage sat behind the house. Both doors were locked. Upstairs there was no answer to the chief's knock. Shit! How much more of this did I have to take? How much more could I take? A tear ran down my cheek. I used my hand to wipe it away, then quickly returned that hand to my pocket. My godchild might be on the other side of that upstairs door, but I had less chance of getting inside than I had at the Pirate Cove's with its resident manager.

The chief knocked again, this time louder. Still no answer. Help, however, wasn't far away. All of us turned when a woman spoke from next door. A low hedge separated the properties.

"Mary Ann's not home, Chief," said the woman from the safety of a door opening against the wind. She wore a housecoat and had to raise her voice for the chief to hear her.

"I thought Kathy Strickland lived here, Kitty."

"She does. I thought you were checking on Mary Ann. I told her not to go out in this weather, but Mary Ann never misses her weekly bridge game. What did you want with her?"

"Kathy Strickland," said the chief starting down the stairs. "I have some people here looking for her."

"When did she leave?" I asked, crossing the driveway to stand near the low hedge so I wouldn't have to raise my voice.

"Kathy left early this morning, like I told that other woman."

"What other woman?"

"Why the one who came looking for Kathy. She was here twenty minutes ago. I told her how to find Old Fort. She wrote down the directions and went out there."

"Was she a heavy woman with black hair, good skin, and lightly made up?" Behind me Largo clumped down the stairs.

"I can't say how heavy she was because she had on one of them hunting jackets, you know, with the thick quilting and sweat pants, but what you're describing about her face—it was that woman, and she was a rather large woman. What's the problem, Happy? Something wrong with Kathy?"

"No," I interjected, "with the woman you described."

"Well, all I did was tell her how to get to Old Fort. Kathy thinks she can find the ruins of another one of the forts, but everybody knows the coastline has changed too much over the years."

"Where is this Old Fort?" I asked the chief.

"I'll show you."

"And in a jiffy."

"Miss Chase, now don't be going on—"

Taking him by the arm, I ushered him down the driveway. "I understand very well what's going on. Louise Moultrie has gone to Old Fort to kill Kathy Strickland. She had help setting it up, from those private eyes I mentioned earlier. If you don't want Kathy's murder on your hands, you'll use your blue light to get us out there and fast."

15

I'll say one thing for the chief. When he saw a lawsuit looming on the horizon, he got to stepping. Largo flipped on his blue light and worked the radio in his car. Chad had trouble keeping up with him as the cruiser rocketed through town and out into the country.

The Lost Colony is performed in an open-air theater with rows of benches permanently built into a bowl-shaped arena. The theater has burned to the ground more than once, been washed out to sea more than that, and each time loyalists from the surrounding area and parts beyond show up to rebuild the backdrop, which looks like a fortified wall of a wooden fort.

The wall's fort, however, could not defend against the icy blast from the Atlantic. Despite being built close to the ground, Chad's 'vette felt like it was being shoved back and forth across the road as we raced past the bowl-shaped arena near the ocean. Why Parnell would bring a baby out in this weather I could not understand. Then, with a sinking heart I remembered—I'd been the one to encourage Babe to take Megan outside as long as the baby was bundled up.

I was going to kill the bitch as soon as I found her. And if the chief or my boyfriend thought they were going to stop me, they had another think coming. What was it Dads said? Revenge is a dish best eaten cold. In this weather I'd be scoffing it down.

As we passed the arena, a sedan approached us from the other direction, and Chief Largo slowed down to block its path. The sedan tried to veer away and ran off the road into the bleachers, thumping down row after row until coming to a stop. More work for the volunteers next spring. After seeing a man step out of the car and collapse across one of the bleachers, we moved on. We could see the chief radioing for someone to pick up one of Louise Moultrie's private eyes.

Old Fort was down the road about two miles and it was one of those grassy areas in a clearing where ridges had once made up the sides of an earthen fort. This one was pretty typical. It had been built near the water, but the undergrowth had been allowed to take over the surrounding area. Why not? *The Lost Colony* was the big moneymaker around here.

Chad pulled into the gravel parking lot between the chief's cruiser and another car. There was a second parked a few yards away. I was the first one out, leaving the passenger-side door open and striding through a wooden rail fence, then onto the grounds of the grassy fort, pushing myself up the ten-foot, sloping earthen hill.

When I topped the side of the fort, I saw no one in the bowl-shaped interior. I got my bearings when a shot rang out on the far side of the fort's wall. Sucking it up, I unbuttoned my greatcoat and ran down the wall into the center of the grass-covered fort. Then, using my momentum, I kept running up the far wall and over to the other side. The chief fell behind and Chad stumbled, then tumbled into the middle of the fort. So I was all alone when I faced Babe Parnell. Chad hollered for me to stop, as did the chief. No way. This was between me and her.

Babe was dressed for the weather in a heavy navy blue coat, and I recognized her even though long blond hair trailed from under the ski cap she wore. She was bending over Louise Moultrie, who lay in a heap at the bottom of the earthen wall.

"Now I hope you're happy," she was saying to the prone woman at her feet.

I barely had enough strength to start downhill, then gravity took over. I was running full speed when I threw myself into the bitch, knocking her away from Moultrie and sending Parnell sprawling toward the tree line.

When she stopped rolling, she looked up to see what had hit her. "Susan . . . what are you doing here?"

I'd landed near Louise Moultrie, and her heavy clothing made it hard to tell if the dean was still breathing. "You invited me . . . don't you remember?"

"I invited you?"

Babe got shakily to her feet, then stumbled toward me. She had no weapon. That was good. All I could manage was getting to my hands and knees.

"Why would I invite you to *The Lost Colony?* It's not open this time of year."

As Chad and the chief came over the side of the grassy wall of the fort, I moved across the ground on my hands and knees until stopping where Moultrie lay. Gasping for air, I put a couple of fingers to her throat. Moultrie had no pulse. When I rolled her over a gun fell out of her lap.

I looked up at Parnell. "You killed her, didn't you?"

"Susan, how could you say such a thing?"

"When it comes to you, I'd believe anything."

The fucked-up woman shook her head. "I'm not who you think I am. I'm not Babe or Connie. That life didn't work out. I'm a new person: Kathy Strickland. Doctor Deitz said I could rehabilitate myself and I did it—on my own."

Chad and the chief joined us.

"Moultrie's dead, Chief. Babe, or Kathy, or whatever the

hell her name is, killed her."

"What's going on here, Happy?" asked the mystery woman. "Why are you here?"

"We thought you might be in danger, Kathy."

I snorted. "That'd be the day."

"Careful, Suze," said my boyfriend, giving me a hand to my feet. "Let the chief handle this." Chad put an arm around me, sheltering me from the wind, steadying me.

The chief knelt beside the dead woman. A pair of hiking boots were on Moultrie's feet, and around her head, a knitted band to keep her ears warm. Largo touched the woman's throat in the same manner I had and drew the same conclusion. "She's dead, Kathy."

"She came here to kill me, but only killed herself."

"What the hell are you talking about?" That was my voice, ragged, almost at the breaking point, me clutching Chad as much as he clutched me. "You killed her like you killed all the others." I scanned the grounds. "Where's Megan?" I said with what little hope I had left.

"Megan?"

The chief asked, "How did this happen, Kathy?"

"She came here while I was working." Parnell gestured to the other side of the fort. "She said she had evidence that I had killed her daughter. I did nothing of the sort. No one ever accused me of anything except carelessness."

"Carelessness." I shook my head and it felt like the sumbitch was about to explode. I'd finally tracked down this bitch, but she was playing the same fool I'd remembered from Donna Destefani's apartment.

"Kathy," asked Largo, "how did this woman die?"

Parnell pointed in the direction of the far side of the fort. "I was working with my equipment outside the fort when Dean Moultrie walked around the corner. There was a man with her. Dean Moultrie pulled a gun from the pocket of her overcoat and said she was going to shoot me. The man said he wanted no part of that and left. When the dean turned and told the man he had to stay, I ran up the side of the fort, trying to put the wall between me and her. She fired at me and the shot went over my head. Then I ran down into the middle of the fort and out again."

"And?"

"She must've misjudged the hill or something and tripped . . . I guess. I wasn't really watching. I was running for the trees when I heard the gun go off. When I didn't hear her anymore, I came out and looked around. The dean was lying where you see her now."

"You were hunched over her when I topped the hill. You killed her, Babe."

"I didn't do anything of the sort. Dean Moultrie fell on her gun and killed herself."

"It could've happened as she says, Miss Chase. I'll get some people out here to study the crime scene."

"I don't give a damn about that. I want to know where my godchild is." Any moment I'd collapse and lie as limp as Louise Moultrie.

"I don't know where Megan is. Why won't you believe me?"

"You have her hidden somewhere. I just know it!" I took a faltering step toward her. "Tell me where she is!"

"Happy, what's going on? Megan Destefani drowned in a storm at Myrtle Beach along with her mother. Of all people Susan should know that. She's the one who led the search."

Finally I lost it. All I remember was Chad and Largo pulling me off the woman, and I'm proud to say, it took both of them to do it.

We sat on a bench in the police station, me shaking, not from the cold, but from how Babe Parnell continued to run her game on everyone. Why couldn't people see through her lies?

Chad brought me something to drink and a pill to relax my nerves. The drunk in the cell block had been released. His singing was fucking getting on my nerves. Across the room Gloria, the dispatcher, stared at me. I saw this each time I looked up from my trembling hands. I wondered when the pill was going to kick in.

The chief came out of the cell block with Parnell.

I slid forward to the edge of the bench. "What did you find?"

"Miss Chase, remember, you promised."

I bit my lip. That had been the deal Chad had struck after I'd lost my cool and attacked Parnell. I was allowed to be here only if I kept my mouth shut, and I was doing about as well as you would imagine.

Parnell wiped her hand with a cloth. "The test came out negative as I told you it would. I didn't fire a gun today and the test proves that."

"You wore gloves."

"I didn't have my gloves. I'd left them at home."

"Then you really are nuts. In this weather everyone wears gloves."

"Miss Chase, please!"

"Then where are yours, Susan?"

I glanced at my hands. "I—I don't wear them inside."

Parnell smirked. "Maybe in your pocket?"

I let go of the bench long enough to rummage through the pockets of my coat. My gloves weren't there. "I must've left them in Chad's car." The room suddenly moved. What was up with that? The pill was supposed to calm my nerves?

"Then why couldn't I have left mine at home?" asked Parnell.

"On a day like this? You were going to work out there, remember? Her gloves are in the water, Chief. As soon as she killed Moultrie, she tossed them in the water. You'll never find them."

"Miss Chase, please . . . I don't want to order you out of here, but I will."

Everyone was looking at me. Chad, Gloria the dispatcher, Happy Largo, and Babe Parnell. The pressure in my head was enormous and my hands shook. Any moment I would burst into tears. But I wouldn't let this bitch get away with murder. Dead kids could tell no tales, but somehow I had to convince someone that this woman was guilty. And Babe Parnell stood there telling the world Megan had died during the rainstorm with her mother.

That wasn't true. This wasn't the way things were supposed to turn out. I'd tracked down this bitch, built a case against her, one dead kid at a time, and now she was standing in the middle of this police station telling everyone her lies, and everyone believing her.

It wasn't right! It wasn't right at all. I bent over and held my head in my hands. Someone put an arm around me. It didn't help. Whoever it was couldn't hold me tight enough to keep me from falling apart.

16

I woke up in a room—with bars on the windows! "Why am I in jail?"

Chad rose from his chair to stand over my bed. I felt sleepy. They must've given me something.

"You're not in jail, Suze. You're in a hospital."

I glanced at the window again. "A hospital with bars on the windows."

"And locks on the doors." He gripped my hand. "You've suffered a breakdown. You need to rest."

Chad appeared to be the only one who understood I was only temporarily jazzed up. Dads was there—until some man in uniform asked him to leave. Harry wanted to read to me. He said it was the quickest way to recovery.

Mickey DeShields and J.D. Warden arrived and said the job was mine, if I passed my GED and got a clean bill of health from SLED's therapist. I might be in therapy six months to a year. Chad was going to like that, but me, I would've rather nailed Connie Parnell.

Chad's mom arrived, and after reassuring me everything was going to be okay, I wound up in a tight little ball—and stayed there. Why wouldn't these people go away and leave me alone?

Or at least talk about my missing godchild. The thought of Megan brought tears to my eyes. That damn Parnell seemed to have more lives than any damn cat. No one would talk about her, saying everything would be fine and for me to rest and get better.

I don't think I could've ever recovered, ever accepted Chad's proposal of marriage until the night someone slipped into my room, sliding through the narrow opening and closing the door behind her.

I was supposed to be alone. Hell, I wanted to be alone, and for that reason, had retreated to the fetal position, hands over my ears, sheet pulled over me. Still, someone always slept in the chair alongside my bed. Harry was there now, snoring away, leaving me with my thoughts.

I had fucked up! Ol' street-wise Susan Chase had set out to find her godchild and ended up not even being able to prove she was still alive. Megan had died in the storm, like everyone said, and I couldn't pin anything on Connie Parnell. Happy Largo probably let the bitch walk. Still, it would appear I could not get the woman out of my life.

"Susan, you awake?"

It was a girl, maybe a nurse, but I was staying under my frigging sheet, tight as a ball, snug as a bug in a rug. Why do people say that? Do bugs really care where they sack out? I must've fallen asleep because my hands had slipped away from my ears and I could hear the voice.

"Susan?"

Still, I stayed in my safe position where no one and nothing could reach me, not even Chad's proposal of marriage.

"Is it okay for me to come in?" whispered the voice.

When I didn't answer, the voice moved closer. "I've been worried about you. I heard you had a breakdown."

Good God, how much more of this shit did I have to take? Would you *puhhhh-lease* go away so I could get back to sleep? Which was about impossible with Harry snoring in the chair beside me.

"I dropped by to apologize. I thought you, most of all, would understand."

"Understand what?" It was okay to ask questions. I was safe under my sheet.

"About being alone in a world where bad things can happen. How you have to fight for your soul . . . or you'll become nothing more but what others say about you—whether it's good or bad."

I knew that voice.

The therapist said I would allow people, and their voices, into my world when I felt safe again.

Safe in my world! I don't think so. My world was too screwed up and I was paying the price.

"Susan, are you having trouble sleeping? I can have the nurse bring you something. I know how difficult it can be to sleep in this place."

How difficult it can be to sleep in this place! That got me out of the fetal position and from under the sheet. The figure in the darkness stood at the foot of my bed.

"I'm sorry to have bothered you." Suddenly, she hunched over and began to sob, pulling her hands into her chest. "I really am."

Harry stopped snoring. By the time his snoring started again, Connie had straightened up. She had more to say, and I could only sit there and listen. Did the woman have a weapon? In the dark I couldn't tell. Easy enough for the bitch to step over and slice Harry's throat as he lay, head back, snoring away.

"Actually . . . ." Parnell cleared her throat. "No harm was done. All the babies were returned."

I said nothing. I didn't even breathe. The sheet was tight around me from where I had twisted out of the fetal position. I started peeling the fabric off me.

"And I cured myself, just as you are doing." She gestured toward the hallway. "We don't need these silly hospitals, do we? You and I?"

When I didn't reply, her voice lightened. "You know, I think I'm ready to have a baby of my own. I trust myself now."

Finally I could push the sheet down and sit up. "Why don't you, Connie? And when you do, bring her to see me."

"Oh, yes," said the voice, brightening, "and you could be the godparent and we could name the child 'Megan.'"

I had my feet over the side of the bed now. Why this hospital didn't have a panic button near the headboard . . . Duh, Susan, everyone in here is always in a panic. Swallowing hard, I said, "Good idea." My feet were on the floor now.

"You wanted to see Megan again, didn't you? That's what this was all about, wasn't it?"

Even someone suffering a nervous breakdown could hear the change in Parnell's tone of voice. Maybe someone in such a state could hear the change better than most. I gripped the edge of the mattress for leverage.

"Well," she asked, coming around the corner of the bed, "aren't you going to answer?"

I launched myself at her, knocking Parnell away from Harry and to the floor. We landed in a mad tangle and slid across the linoleum floor and into the corner. The sound of Parnell's screams brought orderlies racing down the hall. They found me on top of Parnell with Dads trying to pry me off. He wasn't strong enough, but the two big guys did it and quite easily.

As the light came on, the two lugs held me back. Dads had collapsed in his chair, winded. Parnell stood across the room from me. She wore a hospital gown.

"Miss Chase," demanded one of the orderlies, "what are you doing?"

"Trying to stop this bitch before she kills any more children."

Parnell brushed down her gown. "I'm sorry I upset you, Susan. I just dropped by to see how you were doing."

I tried to shake loose, but the two lugs held on tight. Perhaps a saner approach would work? I stopped struggling.

"Is this woman a patient here?" I asked.

"I assume so," said one of the attendants, "but she's not assigned to this wing."

"Well, it's been nice visiting with you," said Parnell as she crossed in front of me. "But next time I'll bring along an orderly so you can't attack me."

I tried to shake loose, but the two guys held on tight.

"Calm down, Miss Chase. We've been warned—"

"About the wrong gal." I stuck out a foot and tripped Parnell. She fell on her face on the linoleum floor and slid out the door.

Harry staggered to his feet from his chair. "That woman is a patient. Her name is 'Connie Parnell.' She's assigned to the wing for the criminally insane."

The two attendants holding me stared at Harry. One said, "Mr. Poinsett, no one from the criminally insane wing could possibly get over here."

"Of course not," said Parnell, now on her feet and standing in the hallway. She brushed down her gown again. "Now I'll just be returning to my room."

Still in the grip of the orderlies, I asked, "And what would the room number be, Babe?"

"Why 202."

"Room 202?" asked one of the attendants, looking at his companion. "Why that's Mrs. Collins and a nicer woman couldn't be found. She has Alzheimer's."

"Well," said Parnell, from the hallway, "perhaps it was 203 or 204—I really don't remember." She turned to leave. "I can find my own way." And she left with the two orderlies staring at each other.

They didn't stare long, but let go of me and hustled down the hall after her. Dads was on his cell phone calling security, and me, I was exhausted. Going from the fetal position to a more active role was grueling work. As I collapsed back in bed, a siren went off, and if small children were lucky, Connie Parnell would be caught in the lockdown.

"Princess, are you all right?" asked Harry, putting away his phone.

"Feeling better than I have been in a long, long time." I brushed down my own hospital gown. "Harry, since you have your cell phone handy, would you mind calling Chad?"

"Certainly, my dear. I'm sure he'll want to know you're safe."

"Don't tell him about this. He'll learn soon enough. Just tell him 'I accept.'"

"Accept what? Megan's death? The necessity for your confinement here at the hospital?"

I smiled for the first time in a long time and my face welcomed the change. "Tell Chad I accept his proposal of marriage. Tell him 'I do.'"

Harry smiled. "I'm sure he'd rather hear that than anything about Connie Parnell."

Harry punched up the numbers in his cell phone as I lay back with my hands under my head. I stretched out full-length, without any sheet covering me. That would make it easier for my man to get at my bod when he arrived.

When Dead Is Not Enough
A Susan Chase Mystery

About the time we arrived at the motel to make the drug bust, my fellow SLED agent, Mickey DeShields, would've left our boss's car in the parking lot of the pancake house behind the motel. There, Mickey, dressed as a bum, would become a staggering drunk, investigating the contents of the dumpster behind the pancake house, then moving on to the dumpster alongside the Sunnydale Motel.

This was why the bad guys had chosen the room at the end of the L-shaped motel. If they smelled trouble, all they had to do was throw a few bags into their van, leap in, and drive into the rear parking lot of the pancake house. They didn't know that J.D. Warden was parked there to block their escape route.

As Earl Tackett, the cop I was partnered with, turned into the parking lot of the Sunnydale, a van approached from the other direction and turned in right behind us. The van stopped at the office and the driver climbed down. Slipping out the rear was another cop. His job? Baby-sit the manager. Around any dealer's crib you never know who's on the pad.

"Oh, this is nice," I said, glancing at the van. "They were supposed to be here already."

"I'm sure everything will work out just fine, Susan."

Earl Tackett, a sergeant in the Myrtle Beach Police Department, continued to the far end of the parking lot in my jeep and parked in front of the bad guys' unit. The window curtain of the room was pulled back, but only slightly. So we sat there, waiting for our backup still parked at the motel's office. It kind of got on my nerves.

Turning to Tackett, I said, "Slap me."

"What?"

"We've got to distract them."

"Susan, I can't hit a woman."

So I slapped him hard enough to make his teeth rattle. A moment later he returned the favor. After bursting into tears, I begged him to give me some money. He wouldn't.

"Push me out of the jeep. I'm going inside."

"Susan, this wasn't the plan."

I stumbled down from the jeep—the sides were not up as it was the merry month of May—went over to the door of the motel room, and knocked. That got my partner moving.

Down the sidewalk, a maid was catching the late checker-outers. She was also a cop, pushing a cart and looking the part. Another cop baby-sat the remaining maids in the store-room. It was hard to see how anything could go wrong, but that's when things usually do.

Tackett joined me at the door. "I don't like the way you're handling this."

The cop-dressed-like-a-maid glanced at the pool-cleaning cops, whose van had finally moved into position behind us and parked alongside the fence surrounding the pool. Ah, nothing like more than one vehicle and more than one person converging on the same location at the same time.

The pool-cleaning cops were my age, wore jeans, tee shirts, and what looked like headphones for a DiscMan. They got out of the van, arguing over who would climb down into the pool. After that they began to discuss the weather. You'd think they were up for an Oscar.

"It's warming up," said one of them.

"Wait 'til July," said the other, "then you'll really see some heat."

The rest of what they said was lost in the clatter of equipment being hauled out of the van. About now Mickey DeShields should be stumbling across the alley separating the two motels, ready to search the dumpster alongside the Sunnydale.

Tackett gave the door a second knock.

No answer, just some rattling around inside.

They wouldn't be hiding their stash, would they?

No, Susan, but they could be gathering up their Uzis.

The knob turned and the door opened. A pair of blue eyes squinted through the crack, then looked down at me. This had to be the big guy we'd been briefed about: blue eyes and a deep tan. Blond bangs fell across his forehead.

"Yeah—what you want?"

"I—I was told you could . . . I could—"

"We were told to ask for Leon," cut in Tackett.

"What you want with Leon?"

"What the devil you think . . . ?" Tackett tried to look inside but the big guy blocked the way. "Maybe this ain't the right place."

"But—but it's got to be." I shook, then pleaded, "You've got the shit, haven't you?"

The big guy gave me another look, then opened the door. When I tried to go inside, Tackett stopped me.

"You stay out here."

"Earl, I gotta have—"

"Let the girl in," said Ol' Blue Eyes.

Like there was any doubt the blonde wouldn't be allowed inside? I wore cutoffs, a cropped top, a pair of running shoes, and of course, my fanny pack. I went ahead of Tackett into the darkened room.

A wall lamp between the double beds with a towel draped over it gave the room very little light. Any other light came through the space between the curtains or from the bathroom. A second guy sat at a table in the rear of the room with an open briefcase. The lid of the briefcase hid one hand.

When Dead Is Not Enough

With the other hand he smoked a cigarette. The light from the bathroom cast a narrow slice across his shoulder and the table in front of him.

He gave me the once-over as I approached the table. The table had been moved from its usual place near the window to the rear, between the beds and the washbasin. Ol' Blue Eyes stood behind me and alongside Tackett, towering over us. A pistol was jammed into his belt, but it was his arms that drew my attention. This guy could do major damage without any frigging weapon.

"What can we do for you, honey?" asked the guy behind the table.

"Is this the place?" asked Tackett.

"What place, fella?" The second guy's legs were stretched out in front of him and crossed at the ankles under the table. His brown, curly hair hung to his shoulders, and his beard grew thick. He wore jeans and a short-sleeved shirt open at the chest, a gold chain around his neck, and earrings in both ears. Behind the briefcase lay a pistol. I could barely see it, but, hey, when you're in a room full of testosterone, a gal tends to pick up on such things.

I stood near the space between the two double beds, their sheets and covers in a mad tangle. Empty boxes of Chinese takeout sat on the nightstand, as did the motel's telephone. Newspapers had collected between the beds and been trampled underfoot.

Tackett asked, "You guys selling dope or what?"

The big guy ran his hand up and down my arm and goose bumps appeared. A tattoo encircled those biceps: decorative barbed-wire. Sorority girls are fascinated with tattoos when they should be strapping on their running shoes.

"Why you with him?" asked the guy at the table. Leon inclined his head in the direction of Tackett.

"I—I needed a fix."

"Yeah, right, but that still don't answer the question. Why'd you bring him along?"

"She don't sleep with you guys," said Tackett. "She just wants a hit."

The long-legged guy regarded Tackett. "You don't do shit, do you?"

Tackett gestured toward the huge man behind him. "Like your friend here—I juice up," inferring he used steroids.

"But you don't mind your woman doing a little hooking, do you?" asked the guy at the table.

Tackett shrugged.

"Hey, you got the stuff or do we gotta go somewhere else?"

Stepping forward, I saw the briefcase was full of money. Thinking that might be something I shouldn't see, I glanced behind me. It was then that I saw Ol' Blue Eyes pull his pistol. Thrusting it in the small of Tackett's back, he ran the barrel up Tackett's back until the barrel ran into something.

The wire.

"What's this?" The big guy backed away, leveling his weapon at Tackett.

Very slowly, Tackett turned around and, as he did, pulled back his jacket, revealing his shoulder harness. "So I carry. I've got a permit."

"Sure you're not cops?" asked Leon, pulling his legs in under him.

"If I was cops, I wouldn't be here."

Leon stood up behind the table and pointed his weapon at us. "And that might be why you're here."

Tackett turned to Leon, his hands open in surrender. "Hey, you want us out of here, we're gone."

With Leon's pistol on us, the big guy returned to the door and opened it. He saw the maintenance men in the pool area, then stuck his head farther out and looked down the sidewalk where he probably saw the cop-dressed-as-a-maid or perhaps her cart.

Ol' Blue Eyes closed the door. "Nobody out there."

He glanced at the monitor feeding a signal from a minicam on the dashboard of their van. On the black-and-white screen,

When Dead Is Not Enough

the bum continued to dig through the Sunnydale dumpster.

Leon was around the table now, running the barrel of his pistol up and down my arm. It was a fourteen-round little monster that could rip you in half with a single burst, if you could keep the barrel steady.

Tackett stepped toward Leon. "Hey, we didn't come here for—"

A blow to the back of my partner's head knocked him to the floor. Startled, I stepped back. Ol' Blue Eyes had split Earl's scalp open with the butt of his pistol, and because Tackett was bald, you could see his skull until the blood pooled up and began to run down his head.

"Why—why you'd do that?" I didn't have to pretend to shudder.

Ol' Blue Eyes kicked Tackett in the back, then kicked him again. My partner never moved.

"Why are you kicking him?" That should be enough to get the pool-cleaning guys in here.

"Take off your clothes, bitch!" This from Leon.

"No, no!" I backed away, into the space between the double beds. The pool-cleaning guys could hear all this over the wire, couldn't they?

"Honey," Leon said, "get those clothes off. You've got work to do."

"But—but I didn't get my hit."

"And you ain't gonna get one unless you perform." He looked me over from head to toe. "We're leaving tonight. If you're any good we might take you along. Looks like you're built for screwing. Look at them hips."

What a terrible thing to say. Oh well, I've always been rather sensitive about the size of my hips.

Stepping over Tackett, he reached for me.

Where were the pool guys?

The huge guy grabbed my cropped top and tried to pull it off. When he did, I went limp, almost losing my top as I went down. Ol' Blue Eyes had no other choice than to let me slide all the way to the floor.

"Get up, bitch!"

"Please don't hurt me." Where was the frigging backup?

Not a sound from outside.

Oh, well, it looked like we were going to have to do this the old-fashioned way: one bad guy at a time.

ABOUT THE AUTHOR

A member of Mystery Writers of America, Sisters in Crime, and the International Association of Crime Writers, Steve Brown is the author of six Susan Chase mysteries, plus *Radio Secrets,* a novel of suspense about a radio psychotherapist with a secret past; *Black Fire,* the story of a modern-day Scarlett and Rhett facing a church-burning in Southern Georgia; and *Woman Against Herself,* a suspense novel in which a single mom takes on a drug kingpin.

Steve lives with his family in South Carolina. E-mail him about Susan Chase at www.susanchase.com.

If you would like to read more about Susan Chase, please ask for her books by title and number:

Printed in the United States
25583LVS00002B/88-105